Difficult Run

A NOVEL

John Dibble

MARKER OAK

BOOKS™

Washington, DC

For information address Marker Oak Books, 1101 30th Street, N.W., Suite 500, Washington, DC 20007.

www.markeroakbooks.com

Printed in the United States of America.

Library of Congress Control Number: 2013905992

ISBN-13: 978-0-615-79058-9

ISBN-10: 0615790585

BISAC: Fiction / Mystery & Detective / General

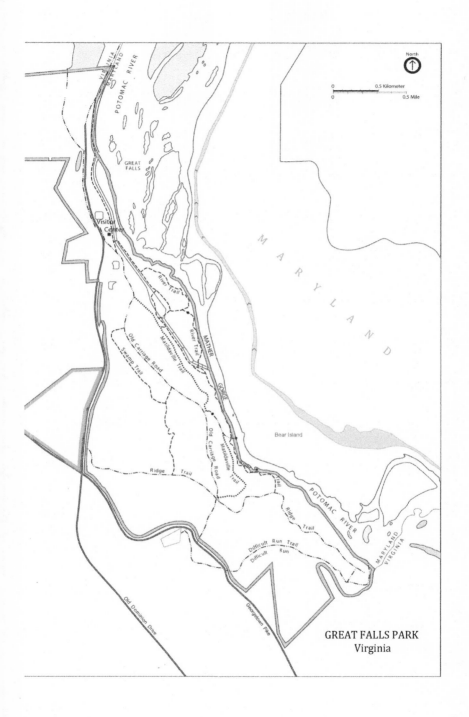

CHAPTER ONE

The curled fingers of the giant hand suddenly thrust out of the low-lying fog as she rounded the turn in the road. A breeze briefly parted the mist and she could see the face of the creature, teeth bared in preface to a primal scream, the other hand just breaking through the soil, seeking a purchase that would allow the enormous body to pull itself from the earth.

She had to run faster, fast enough to pass by the thing before it could rise up and grab her with an outstretched arm, dragging her back into the ground with it. Her breathing quickened, providing needed oxygen for the muscles that would propel her away from danger. Toes pushing harder on the pavement, she increased the length of her stride and felt her body accelerate toward the next turn.

As she passed the three-mile marker on the side of the road, she glanced at her watch which showed an elapsed time of 18:40. Not bad, she thought, doing a fast conversion to a time of around 38:30 for a 10 kilometer run. Considering that the heavy rains in Washington over the past four days had made it impossible to run at all, she was especially pleased with herself. Hains Point, where she was now running, had been completely flooded by the Potomac River, including the open area where the metal sculpture called *The Awakening* was located. She loved the sculpture of a giant emerging from the ground and used it as an artifice in her daily runs, pretending that it was a real creature emerging from the earth and pursuing her. On average, she estimated that the additional push to escape his clutches improved her time by three to five seconds overall.

She had about a mile left to go. Her breathing was measured and deep. The length of her stride remained at the *Awakening* level, although she wasn't sure she could maintain it all the way to Park Police Headquarters. She didn't want to risk injuring herself. Her muscles had been deprived of strenuous exercise for four days and she knew that cramps or worse, ligament tears, were a real possibility.

M.J. Powers was twenty-eight years old, five feet ten inches tall and weighed about one hundred thirty-five pounds, a lot of which was muscle mass. As her mother used to say, she was "all legs." Her mother also used to say that she didn't have much in the "chest department," which, because of her running, was probably just as well since she didn't want the aggravation of dealing with flailing breasts. She wore her light brown hair shoulder length, except when she was running and put it in a ponytail.

It was the beginning of spring 2005. Earlier in the year, she had decided that instead of training for the Marine Corps Marathon in the fall, she would concentrate on improving her time in 5 kilometer and 10 kilometer runs. She had a decent finish in last year's Marathon, but the number of people participating had risen to thirty thousand and the crowding had reduced her enjoyment of the event. She had been forced to think carefully about just why she had become a runner in the first place and had decided that ultimately it was the solitary challenge that kept her at it. Although she could find that challenge running alone, there was also a need to compete at some level, to prove to herself that she could outperform other runners. She just wanted more control over the setting, and masses of marathon runners in a highly-publicized event like the Marine Corps Marathon didn't fill this need. Of course there were other runners in 5K and 10K events, but nothing approaching the size of the Marine Corps event. There were also more of the smaller events in which to compete, and she liked that aspect, too.

She had been so focused on her running that she was unaware of the car rolling along next to her on the left. The passenger-side window rolled down and a voice said, "Hey, Detective Powers, our presence has been requested at Great Falls." It was her partner, Jake Hill.

"Shit, Jake," she said, with obvious irritation in her voice, narrowing her light blue eyes for effect. She continued to run but slowed her pace. "You know I can't just stop. I need to cool down. Give me a couple hundred yards and I'll get in."

"It's OK with me. Just don't let Swain know that I didn't force you into the car," he replied.

Lieutenant Mike Swain was the Commander of the Criminal Investigations Branch, or CIB, their boss and a royal pain in the ass. He made a big deal out of everything, and in the U.S. Park Police that required some real imagination.

"So what are we dealing with?" she asked, still breathing heavily.

"A double homicide. That's about all I know," Jake replied. "They sent some uniformed guys out from our station on the Parkway and Zerk is already on his way there, so maybe he'll have something by the time we get there."

Peter "Zerk" Bensen was the identification technician for their unit. He had acquired the nickname Zerk as a child because his father was an auto mechanic and called him that after the grease fittings used on cars. "That kid's going to be a real slick customer," his father used to say. "Slick as axle grease."

Zerk's father was wrong on a number of counts, not the least being that Zerk was about as far from "slick" as possible. In fact he was the quintessential nerd but, like many nerds, very smart and very good at his job. M.J. also figured that his job had gotten him laid on more than one occasion. She could just imagine the pick-up line in a singles bar: The vacuous twenty-something woman asking "What do you do?" and Zerk casually replying, "Well, I'm a crime scene investigator." The woman exclaiming, "CSI? For real? Like the T.V. show?" He would carefully omit the fact that he worked for the U.S. Park Police to avoid the inevitable references to raccoons and Smokey the Bear. He would probably just say, "Maybe you could come over to my place later and I could tell you about some of the cases I've worked on."

"M.J., time to get in the car," Jake said.

She opened the passenger door with the car still rolling and hopped in. "Take me by Headquarters so I can get my stuff. No time to shower, I suppose, but we'll probably be outdoors and I'll try to stay downwind," M.J. said.

Jake pulled up to the rear entrance of Headquarters and M.J. trotted inside. She splashed cold water on her face and the back of her neck, briefly fussed with her hair and opened the locker that she used when she ran at Hains Point. She reached into her gym bag and found a pair of nylon workout pants, pulled them over her shorts, grabbed her jacket with POLICE printed on the back, donned a dark blue baseball cap with the Park Police emblem on the front, put on her gun belt and grabbed her badge before returning to the car.

As soon as they began moving, Jake turned on the flashing lights. When they cleared the parking lot, he turned on the siren. It was 7:45 a.m., the peak of rush hour in Washington. Although they would be traveling counter to the commuter traffic, he planned to make their trip as short as possible. He crossed the 14th Street Bridge, took the ramp onto the George Washington Memorial Parkway—known to everyone as "the GW"—and headed north. There was a lingering fog that blocked the early morning sun and reduced visibility to a few hundred yards.

Dispatch came on the radio to tell them that Eagle One, the Park Police helicopter, was awaiting clearance to take off and should be on the scene in about thirty minutes.

At the end of the GW, he turned right onto Georgetown Pike, a winding two-lane road that followed the same path as the wagon trail used in Colonial times. There was bumper-to-bumper traffic in the other lane and the twisting road made it necessary to reduce their speed. After about four miles, they entered a series of cutback turns along the side of some steep hills. Rounding the last of the turns, they saw an area below them on the left where the fog was illuminated by blue, red and yellow flashing lights.

"This must be the place. It looks like a police convention," Jake said, turning left through the oncoming traffic into a parking area.

At the entrance a large wooden sign, stained dark red with yellow letters, said DIFFICULT RUN.

CHAPTER TWO

M.J. had been to Great Falls Park a few times when she was assigned to the Patrol Branch out of the GW Station. It was one of the most scenic areas in the Washington region. The falls themselves consisted of jutting rocks that caused the Potomac River to cascade over a drop of almost a hundred feet. There were several overlooks, a spacious picnic area, a Visitor Center, and several miles of nature trails. She had always entered the park through its main entrance, which she recalled was about a half mile farther on Georgetown Pike. The Difficult Run entrance was new to her. She assumed that it was named for a stream or creek, which in Virginia is called a "run."

Jake pulled into an empty space in the parking lot. A Fairfax County police officer came over and shook his hand, then M.J.'s. "Hi, my name's John Crocker," he said. "This lot is technically our jurisdiction, but the crime scene is in the park, which makes it yours. Just let us know how we can help." He pointed to a car half hidden under a copse of trees and cordoned off with yellow tape. "That appears to be the victims' car over there." He pointed to a second car. "The other car belongs to the woman who found the bodies. She's over there whenever you want to interview her, but she's pretty shaken up at this point."

"Did you run the tags on the victims' car?" M.J. asked.

"Sure did," he replied. "It's registered to a couple in McLean, probably the parents of one of the boys."

"Boys?" M.J. asked.

"Yeah, two of 'em. Trail bikers. See the rack on the back of the car," Crocker said, looking toward the vehicle.

M.J. noted the rack and asked, "Have the parents been notified?"

"Not yet," he replied. "We wanted to wait until you gave us the word."

"Thanks," M.J. said. "We'll try and do that as soon as we can."

Crocker pointed to the far end of the lot. "You'll need to follow that trail about three hundred yards to the beginning of the trail in the park. It follows the stream and it's muddy as hell because of the rain. You might want to take your flashlights too, because of the fog," he said.

Jake reached into his car, retrieved two flashlights and handed one to M.J. They started walking across the parking lot and reached the trailhead at the far side. Once they were out of earshot, M.J. said, "So much for any footprints or tire marks from the parking lot. It looks like the entrance to a stadium on a rainy day." She shined her flashlight down on the trail. "Not much better here," she added. "Christ, I wish they'd limited access until Zerk could look around."

The stream was still swollen from the recent rain. It had obviously gone over its banks during the heavy rain, as evidenced by the trail from the parking lot. "He wasn't kidding when he said it was muddy," Jake said. "So much for my shined shoes."

"Stop complaining," M.J. replied. "I'm wearing my new running shoes that cost a hundred bucks."

Whole trees had washed up next to the trail, which was deeply rutted in several places. The access trail ended and there was a steep path up to the main trail. Another Fairfax County officer was standing there and motioned them to the right, saying, "The bodies are about fifteen or sixteen hundred yards down that way." M.J. glanced to the left and could see the lights from the cars on Georgetown Pike.

The main trail was in much better shape and wider. Almost immediately, they could hear the fast moving water below to their right. As the trail became steeper, the sound of the stream became less audible and they sensed that it was becoming farther and farther below them. Because of the low-lying fog, it was impossible to tell how high they were above Difficult Run, but M.J. thought it could easily be fifty feet or more.

They moved slowly because of the fog, swinging their flashlights from side to side to make sure they didn't step off the edge of the trail and fall down the slope to the stream. After several minutes, the trail became level and they rounded a long sweeping curve. They began to hear voices up ahead. A few minutes later, they could see what appeared to be flashlights moving around in the fog.

They ducked under the yellow crime scene tape that had been placed across the trail and continued toward a group of five people about fifty feet farther down the trail. There were three uniformed Park Police officers, Zerk Bensen and a park ranger.

"What've you got, Zerk?" M.J. asked.

"Well, no footprints on the ground I've covered so far. This trail is compacted gravel and I really don't expect to find any. I've taken a few photos but I want to wait 'til this fog lifts so I can get better quality. You guys need to come look at the bodies," he said, handing M.J. and Jake sets of latex gloves. "Stay behind me. I haven't swept the whole area."

They followed Zerk down the trail and around a slight bend. Ahead, M.J. could see two beams of light shining into the fog, one straight up and one at an angle.

Another crime scene tape was stretched across the trail. Zerk lifted it for them and said, "Stay close. You're not going to fucking believe this."

As they approached the two bodies, M.J. could see that the lights were attached to the bikers' helmets. The bodies were about ten feet apart and the trail bikes were in front of each body.

M.J. shined her flashlight down on the first body. The boy was staring up into space, eyes wide open. She swung her light to the second body. Same thing. Eyes wide open, staring slightly to the side. She started to move the light back to the first body again, when she realized that something about the two bodies wasn't right.

It took a moment for the horrible incongruity to register in her mind. The heads of both boys were staring up, but their torsos were chest down on the trail, palms flat as if they were getting ready to do push-ups.

"My God!" M.J. exclaimed. "Their heads have been turned around on their bodies."

CHAPTER THREE

The three of them knelt down by the first body. The boy's neck was badly bruised and there were abrasion marks on his chin and cheeks, most likely from the strap on the helmet. They moved to the second body and found the same bruises and abrasions. The two trail bikes didn't show any signs of damage.

"It looks like whoever did this jumped the first rider, broke his neck and then took out the other one the same way," Zerk said. "The bikes just continued moving without the riders."

"Whoever it was would have to be really fast to kill them both," Jake said. "It looks like the boys might have been trying to get away and got pulled off their bikes from behind."

"Either the killer was really fast or there was more than one," M.J. said. "Get us some good pictures, Zerk."

"Will do," Zerk said. "From the look of things, that may be about all we have in terms of evidence. I'll take the helmets and bikes back to the lab but I'll be surprised if there are any usable prints."

Zerk led them back up the trail from the crime scene and they rejoined the others. M.J. approached the park ranger, who held out his hand. "I'm the site manager for the park," he said. "My name is Randall McMillan, but call me Dodd. Most people do."

"What do you think happened here, Dodd?" she asked.

"Well, it looks like these kids came into the park after dark. We close the main gate then, but you can still get in through Difficult Run. Bikers aren't allowed on a lot of the trails in the park, so they come in at night this way and go up into the main part of the park. I'd guess they were coming back down off the Ridge Trail and whoever killed them was down here at the bottom on Difficult Run," he said.

"Is there any way out of here other than the trail from the parking lot?" M.J. asked.

"Well, they could have gone up the Ridge Trail and cut through the forest to the main entrance road or doubled back to the parking lot for Difficult Run," Dodd said.

"Can you check with your folks to see if anyone has come through the entrance gate or been in the main part of the park this morning?" she asked.

"I'll check, but the main park has been closed for two days due to the high water and there wouldn't be any way for someone to get in or out of there on foot," he said, adding, "We can't even get to our offices in the Visitor Center."

"If the park is under water, how were these boys able to ride their bikes on the trails?" she asked.

"Well, they could ride the Ridge Trail and the trails on this end toward Difficult Run because it doesn't usually flood during high water. You see, the basin below the falls is like the mouth on a funnel and Mather Gorge downstream is like the stem. The water backs up at the entrance to the gorge and comes over the cliffs around the basin and into the main part of the park," he said, putting his hands together like a funnel.

"How about the river?" M.J. asked.

"The river is so dangerous right now that even kayakers would get sucked under if they hit a rock and a swimmer would have no chance at all," he said.

"Then whoever did this may still be in the park," she said.

"Sure could be. There's lots of places to hide," he replied.

"Please ask your folks to keep an eye out and let us know right away if they see anybody," M.J. said and started walking up the trail toward the parking lot. She stopped to talk to the three uniformed Park Police officers, all of whom she knew from her days with the Patrol Branch.

"One of you needs to stay here to secure the trail while Zerk does his job. We could probably get by with one of you in the parking lot to secure the area where the victims' car is parked and the other can go back on patrol duty," she said and added, with a perceptible smile on her face, "I know how much you love patrolling the GW, so you can draw straws to see who does what."

The pilot of Eagle One came on her handheld radio. It was circling over the park but had limited visibility, even with its infrared camera. "We'll stay on station until the fog lifts and then we should be able to get a better look," the pilot said.

M.J. and Jake made their way back to the parking lot and found Officer Crocker from the Fairfax County Police.

"We think the murderer or murderers may have escaped on foot," M.J. said to Crocker.

"We've got cars patrolling all of the perimeter roads," Crocker responded. "I'll let them know that our suspects may be on foot."

"We're going to leave one of our guys down the trail to help secure the area. There are two others coming back here and one of them can take care of the area around the car," M.J. said.

"Well, we've got to control the entrance to this parking lot anyway, since it's Fairfax County property, so we could probably keep an eye on the car too," Crocker replied.

"We'll leave our guy, just to help out," she said. "Also, if you could notify the families, it would be a big help. Probably a good idea to be sketchy on the details right now, though. Maybe tell them the boys were killed in a biking accident. We'll be talking to them later and can fill in some details, but I want to wait until we have some more information. Same thing goes for the press," she added.

"What about the Medical Examiner?" Crocker asked.

"Let's wait until our technician finishes before we call the M.E. He shouldn't be much longer," M.J. responded.

"Got it," Crocker replied. "By the way, one of our cars picked up some coffee and doughnuts. They're sitting on the hood of my car over there. Help yourself."

"Thanks," M.J. said. "I'll let my partner know."

While M.J. was talking to Crocker, Jake had been interviewing the woman who had discovered the bodies. Her name was Mary Stevens and she appeared to be in her mid-fifties, with short graying hair, an intelligent-looking face and an air of self-assurance. She was sitting in her car with her dog Rambles, a yellow Labrador retriever who did not appear to have missed many meals.

"Rambles and I walk Difficult Run every morning just after sunrise," she said. "There was fog on some parts of the trail when we started, but we know it so well that it seemed safe to go ahead. We usually go all the way down to the river, but right after we rounded the bend about halfway there, Rambles started growling and wouldn't go any farther. I could see two lights shining up in the air on down the trail and thought somebody might be in trouble. I called out, but nobody answered.

"Well, I couldn't get Rambles to move, even when I put on his leash and tugged. I finally just tied him to a tree and started on down the trail by myself. When I got close to where the lights were shining, I took out a little flashlight that I carry on my belt so I could get a better look. That's when I saw those two boys on the ground.

"I knew they were dead. They weren't moving and had horrible expressions on their faces. I'll never forget those expressions. I just hurried back up the trail, got Rambles and headed to my car as fast as I could. I had left my cell phone there and I called 911 right away."

"Did you see anyone else on the trail or in the parking lot?" Jake asked.

"Not a soul," she replied.

"Did you ever find out what was bothering Rambles?" Jake asked.

"I think he just sensed that those dead boys were down there and got spooked. Dogs are funny that way, you know," she said. "What happened to them, anyway? An accident of some sort?"

"We're still investigating it, but thanks for your help. I've got your phone number and we may be back in touch if we have any questions," Jake replied as he reached into the car and gave Rambles a pat on the head. "Good boy," he said.

M.J. was over by the boys' car and Jake joined her there. They ducked under the crime scene tape, pulling on latex gloves as they went. M.J. reached out and tried the door handle. "Locked, of course," she said. "The keys are probably in one of the boy's pockets. Let's wait and see if Zerk has them."

The car, an older model Toyota, was blocked from view from the road by the trees. Judging from the beer cans and condoms littering the area, it appeared to be a popular parking place for teenagers.

Jake filled her in on his conversation with Mary Stevens.

"We can't do much more until Zerk is finished," M.J. said. "The Fairfax County guys got some coffee and doughnuts," she added, pointing toward Crocker's patrol car. "Go ahead and get some. I'll be over in a minute."

M.J. walked around the parking lot imagining the sequence of events: *The boys would have arrived, unloaded their bikes from the rack, rested them against the car, put on their helmets and started for the trail. Was there anyone else in the lot? Did they talk to them? Perhaps there were other trail bikers looking to enter Great Falls Park after hours. If so, was it someone they knew or a stranger? Mary Stevens said there were no other cars in the lot when she arrived just after sunrise, so anyone else who had been there had probably left before dawn.*

She walked over to the patrol car where a group of officers were drinking coffee and munching on doughnuts. Jake was standing off to the side and as she approached he pulled a pack of cigarettes out of his pocket, took one out, and lit it.

"I thought you quit," she said, showing some annoyance.

"I pretty much did, but this seemed like a situation that called for a cigarette," he replied.

"Every situation is one that calls for a cigarette if you let it be," she said reprovingly and walked over to get a cup of coffee.

Jake's smoking was just one of a series of minor irritations that seemed to have recently become more of a problem for her. It also occurred to her that they had been dating seriously for almost two years and that finding fault with him was just a way of justifying her own fear of commitment.

She enjoyed her freedom and had sometimes chafed at Jake's attempts to make their relationship grow into something more permanent. He had wanted her to move in with him, an idea that she had steadfastly resisted. Although they slept together regularly, it wasn't the same as living together and she wanted to maintain her own apartment as a refuge and expression of her individuality. He had even brought up the subject of marriage more than once, but she had dismissed it first with "We haven't known each other long enough" and more recently with "I'm not ready."

She also had to admit that there were a lot of things that continued to attract her to Jake. First of all, he was very handsome. He was about her height and in very good shape, which was important to her. He kept his dark brown hair reasonably short and had piercing brown eyes that she found quite sexy. He was also very thoughtful and affectionate, almost to a fault.

Her reflections on her personal life were interrupted by a call on her radio. It was Eagle One. The fog had dispersed enough to allow use of its infrared camera.

"The only thing we're seeing are some people down the trail, which I assume are our folks," the pilot reported. "We looked at the forest all the way down to the main part of the park. Nothing there but some deer," he added.

She asked the pilot to look along the perimeter roads and check back with her. As soon as she had finished talking to the pilot, Zerk came on the radio. "All finished here, but I'll need some help getting out the bicycles and evidence bags," he said.

M.J. confirmed that Zerk had found the keys to the boys' car and then walked over to Officer Crocker, who was talking to Jake and Dodd McMillan.

"Any way to get in there with a vehicle?" she asked.

"I'd say the best we'll be able to do is send a four-wheeler down the trail to the place where it narrows," Crocker replied. "You'll need to haul everything to that point, including the bodies. I'll contact the Fire and Rescue unit in Great Falls Village. Should I contact the Medical Examiner, too?" he asked.

"Yeah, go ahead on both counts," M.J. said. She walked over to the uniformed Park Police officer in the parking lot. "They're going to bring in a four-wheeler," she said. "You'll need to follow it down the trail and help with getting the evidence up to it; same with the bodies for the M.E."

As M.J. joined Jake and the others, Eagle One came back on the radio. "We're looking along the perimeter roads now. No sign of anyone there or in the forest. Do you want us to remain on station?" the pilot asked.

M.J. looked at Jake and said, "I don't see any reason to keep them around, do you?" He shook his head.

"Eagle One, go on back and thanks for your help," she said into the radio.

She turned to Dodd McMillan and asked, "Are the horses for the mounted unit assigned to the park in the flooded area or can we get riders to them?"

"The horses are kept in a stable off the entrance road to the park. Should be able to get to them without a problem. In fact, they can ride from there through the forest to the area around Difficult Run," he replied.

M.J. called the GW Station on her radio and asked them to send riders.

"I'm beginning to think we're not going to find anyone," she said to Jake, "but I want to try everything we can."

CHAPTER FOUR

They were sitting in Lieutenant Mike Swain's office at the Anacostia Station in Washington where the Criminal Investigations Branch was headquartered. Swain was behind his desk and they were sitting in the two fake leather chairs that had been carefully placed in front of his desk with a full view of the wall behind him, which showcased his various certificates and awards.

"I'm leaving this case with you guys," Swain said. "M.J., I want you to take the lead. Jake has several other cases pending, but he'll be available for backup. This is a big deal case, so give me regular updates. That's it for now."

As they rose to leave, Swain said, "M.J., stay for a minute. I've got some ideas I want to discuss with you."

She sat back down and feigned attentiveness, although she was still processing the images from the murder scene in her mind. Even now, twenty-four hours later, they were disturbingly vivid and horrific.

"So, you may be wondering why I'm assigning this case to you, huh?" Swain asked.

"I hadn't given it much thought, but now that you mention it, I am a little surprised that you didn't give it to someone with a little more seniority and experience," she replied.

"Well, seniority and experience don't really matter on this one. First of all, we don't have that many detectives with homicide experience because the Park Police doesn't see that many homicide cases—certainly not like this one," he said. "No, there are two reasons I'm giving you the case. First, only somebody smart has any chance of figuring out who did it, and you're one of the smartest people in the unit. The other reason is that I doubt anyone else would even want it because it may never be solved at all. Nobody likes unsolved cases. They look bad on everybody's record."

"Well, I appreciate the opportunity," M.J. said, thinking to herself that Swain was more concerned about *his* record than hers. If the case was never solved, he would have a scapegoat; if it was, he would gladly take the credit.

Of course, there were homicides in national parks— several hundred since she had been on the force—but the Park Police didn't handle all of them. That was because they only had units in three locations: Washington, D.C, New York, and San Francisco. Even with that, they often had limited jurisdiction over homicides. Washington was a prime example: Homicides on federal park land within the District of Columbia were the exclusive jurisdiction of the Metropolitan Police. Great Falls Park, on the other hand, was the exclusive jurisdiction of the Park Police.

In addition, some high-profile homicides in national parks had been handled by the FBI at the request of the National Park Service because of the limited resources of the Park Police. The serial murders in Yosemite National Park in 1990 and the murder in 1996 of two women campers on the Appalachian Trail were good examples.

"Are we going to keep this one to ourselves?" she asked Swain.

"For now," Swain replied. "I don't want to ask for help from the FBI or the local police unless we absolutely have to. Let's see how it plays out."

"How about offering a reward for information?" she asked.

"That's certainly on the table, but let's see what you come up with first," he said. "That's all for now, but keep me posted."

She left his office and went back to her cubicle, which faced Jake's.

"So, did you and Swain finish your private discussion?" he asked. "Anything I should know about?"

"Just the usual bullshit," she answered. "Of course, if it goes south, he'll blame it on me. But you'll probably be able to stay clear since you're just backup." She smiled.

"I'm really not trying to stay clear, M.J.," he said. "Keep me in the loop."

"OK," she said. "I'm going back out to the park. Dodd McMillan said he'd give me a tour. May need your help later to follow up on any leads."

"Just let me know," he said.

CHAPTER FIVE

It took M.J. about twenty minutes to drive from Anacostia Station to Great Falls Park. She passed the parking lot at Difficult Run and, about a half mile later, turned into the main entrance. It was about another mile to the gate on a road lined with tall trees that cast dark shadows in the late morning sun. Below, to the right, she could see an expanse of flat land that seemed to melt into heavy forest on all sides, with an occasional trail visible through the foliage.

She showed her badge and was waved through by the ranger at the entrance station. The Visitor Center was just past an open grassy field dotted with picnic tables. The heavy rain and flooding had left large puddles of water over the entire area.

She parked her car in the restricted lot adjacent to the Visitor Center, a clay-colored block building with a cedar shingle roof and ascending ramps on each end. She entered through the door to the ground level where the administrative offices were located.

It wasn't hard to find the office marked "Site Manager – Randall D. McMillan." The door was open and Dodd was sitting behind a long table that served as his desk. It was cluttered with papers from end to end and the only illumination was an old-fashioned banker's lamp with a green glass shade. The walls were lined with bookshelves, some of which contained worn leather-bound volumes that lay on their sides. There were several historical pictures of the park on the wall, including some of areas under water.

M.J. was able to get a better look at Dodd now than the day before at the murder scene. He appeared to be in his early fifties, with close-cropped hair that was turning gray at the edges. His skin was tanned and leathery, undoubtedly from spending a lot of time outside. As he stood up from his desk, she could see that he was trim and obviously in good shape.

"Hope you brought some comfortable walking shoes," he said, removing a pair of reading glasses.

She pointed to the Merrell hiking shoes she was wearing and said, "Ready for my tour of the park."

M.J. looked at two framed pictures on one of the shelves. They were of a woman in her late forties and a younger woman perhaps in her early twenties. M.J. pointed at the pictures and asked, "Is that your wife and daughter?"

"Yes," Dodd replied. "My wife passed away four years ago from cancer. My daughter lives in Wyoming now and it looks like she may be getting married soon. Who knows, a few years from now I may have some pictures of grandchildren up there too."

"I'm sorry to hear about your wife," M.J. said. "That must have been very difficult for you and your daughter."

"It was," he replied, "but my wife fought a good fight to the very end and it made my daughter and me strong, whether we liked it or not. She made us promise that we would go on with our lives and not let her death drag us down. We've both tried to honor that promise, but it hasn't always been easy for either of us. Every year that passes, though, seems to put things more in perspective and that helps."

They left the Visitor Center and started down a wide path that paralleled the river and the remains of the Patowmack Canal, which had been constructed in the late eighteenth century. There were two overlooks from which visitors could get a panoramic view of the falls.

As they turned into the second overlook, Dodd said "A lot of people never get farther than this area. They come to see the falls and maybe have a picnic. The park is much larger—about eight hundred and eighty acres altogether—and runs for four and a half miles from its northern end to Difficult Run at its southern end. We're going to follow the river all the way down to Difficult Run and then loop back along some of the interior trails."

M.J. had seen the falls before, but she was still taken by the majestic view and the raw power of millions of gallons of water cascading over the jagged rocks. Several kayakers were maneuvering the roiled water at the base of the falls, retreating to calmer pools in rocky coves, only to return to the challenge of paddling against the strong current. Everywhere were signs warning visitors not to climb the steep rocks and not to enter the water.

Dodd pointed to one of the warning signs and said, "You know even with all these signs, we lose between eight and twelve people a year out here. They think the river looks real calm at the base of these rocks but don't realize there's a current just below the surface that will drag you under in an instant. The Fire and Rescue team in Great Falls Village saves some of them, but a lot of them we never find at all.

The current takes them down and pins them against a rock on the bottom and they never come up. Sometimes the bodies show up way down river or in the Chesapeake Bay, but not for weeks or months."

"What about the kayakers?" M.J. asked.

"That's a different story," Dodd said. "They all wear life vests and most of them are pretty experienced. We work with them on safety issues and they're real good about warning people away from the water. They've even helped rescue a few visitors that have fallen in. In the time I've worked here, we've only lost one kayaker."

As they left the overlook, M.J. stopped to look at a tall pole that had markers to record the highest floods in the park.

"The flood in '36 was the granddaddy of them all," Dodd said, pointing to the topmost mark. "Came out of nowhere and put this whole area under more than ten feet of water. Of course, this wasn't part of the national park system then. It was privately owned by the Great Falls and Old Dominion Railroad. For a long time, it had a trolley line that ended at a station at the entrance to the park. There was also a road for cars and carriages and the like. The trolley line is long gone, but the road is still here. In fact, we'll be coming back on part of it when we finish your tour."

M.J. looked around the open area and tried to imagine what it would look like under that much water. "How often does the park flood?" she asked.

"We get flooding almost every spring when the snow in the mountains west of here starts to melt, or if there's been a lot of rain in a short amount of time," Dodd said. "The river has to reach around twelve feet above flood stage before it comes over the edge of the basin here at the falls, but it doesn't take that much for it to come over the edge along Mather Gorge. Remember what I said about it being like the stem of a funnel?"

M.J. remembered the analogy. "So do you have to close the trails downriver when that happens?" she asked.

"We close the River Trail all the way along the gorge. Just too dangerous to let anybody in there when the water is coming up the side of the gorge," he replied.

"What about Difficult Run?" she asked.

"Don't need to close it. The gorge opens up into a valley down there and the high water dissipates, but it's still flowing really fast and is dangerous as hell," he said. "That's why I said it looked like those boys had gone down Difficult Run and then cut over on the Ridge Trail so they wouldn't encounter any of the flooding."

They walked down a wide path lined with towering sycamore trees that skirted the picnic area. Dodd turned left onto a narrower trail that led toward the river. "This will take us down to the River Trail along Mather Gorge," he said.

The trail wound through some heavy underbrush and was punctuated with puddles of water from the recent flooding. They came out of the foliage into an open area with large jutting rocks and M.J. could see the cliff on the Maryland side of the river and hear the water rushing through the narrow passage below.

They followed the trail between large outcroppings of moss- and lichen-covered rocks until they came to an open area where they could see the gorge in both directions. M.J. walked to the edge and looked down. The fast-moving water was splashing against the rocky walls on both sides of the gorge and in the middle there were large whirlpools that seemed to appear and disappear in the current.

"The river is still up here," Dodd said. "It normally runs about seventy-five feet below the edge here, but it will take a few days before it calms down."

They walked another half mile until they came to a barricade warning that the trail ahead had washed out.

"We'll need to make a detour here," Dodd said. "This part of the River Trail washes out just about every time there's any flooding and we haven't figured out a way yet to keep it from happening."

They turned right and followed a path that emerged into an open area where massive stone walls lined canal locks that descended in steps to the south. "These are more than 200 years old," Dodd said. "It always amazes me that they are in such good shape. It also amazes me that they were able to build them in the first place. Some of those stones weigh a couple of tons and they all had to be cut by hand and then moved into place using mule teams. Quite an engineering feat."

Pointing to the right, he said, "Up that way are the ruins of the town of Matildaville. During the time the canal was being built and then when it was in operation, it was a bustling community. There's not much left now, just some stone foundations and part of a chimney."

They followed the River Trail south, paralleling the gorge, and then went up a steep incline that had cross-timbers to prevent erosion. M.J. noticed that this part of the park felt more isolated. The trail was less improved and the overhanging trees and massive rock outcroppings gave it an ominous quality that intensified as they hiked farther into the deep forest that covered the hillside.

"These hills are what limit the flooding to the parts of the park that aren't right along the river. They're also what protects Difficult Run," Dodd said, pointing to the south.

They reached the top of the hill and the trail intersected with another trail. "This is the Ridge Trail and we can follow it all the way to Difficult Run," he said. "This area is probably where the boys were biking before they were killed."

The trail leveled along the top of the hill and wound its way through the foliage until it began to slope down sharply over large rocks. It ended at Difficult Run and M.J. recognized the section where they had found the bodies. In the daylight, she could better recreate the scene in her mind. The descent on the Ridge Trail was quite steep and she guessed the boys would have been going very fast before they reached Difficult Run. They had probably planned to turn right and head back to their car in the parking lot. If someone was waiting for them at the bottom, it would have forced them to go left, not right. They had been found less than fifty yards in that direction.

"Let's go down toward the river," Dodd said, walking in the direction the boys had gone.

A few hundred yards later, they reached the end of Difficult Run where the stream emptied into the Potomac River south of Mather Gorge.   There was an otherworldly quality to the scene.   High cliffs framed a wide basin with the river swirling past as it traversed the bends in the river. Viewing it, she thought that it was hard to believe this was only a few miles outside the urban setting of the nation's capital.   It looked more like some undiscovered place in the far west.

They walked back up Difficult Run to the crime scene. M.J. stopped and looked around at the steep hills to the north and the escarpment to the south that bordered the stream some twenty feet below.   The trail was not very wide at this point, maybe eight feet.

The killer or killers would probably have hidden on the hillside just up from the place where the Ridge Trail meets this trail and then jumped down to intercept and attack the boys, M.J. thought. *But why here?   Perhaps because it was so remote and the chances of being discovered so unlikely. That meant that they had some familiarity with the park and especially with Difficult Run.*

"Let's head back to your office," she said. "I think I've seen all I need to for now."

They hiked back up the Ridge Trail and then followed it in the opposite direction from the way they had come until it intersected with a wide gravel road. "This is the Old Carriage Road," Dodd said. "It's used a lot by runners, horseback riders, and bikers."

They followed the Old Carriage Road back to the main part of the park and then cut across to the Visitor Center. When they entered Dodd's office, M.J. looked at her watch. They had been gone almost three hours. "How far do you think we just hiked?" she asked.

"All told, I'd say about eight or nine miles," he replied, adding, "We actually made pretty good time."

M.J. sat across from his desk. "Does anyone stay in the park at night?" she asked.

Dodd hesitated and looked down at his hands. "Well ... not officially," he replied.

"What do you mean *not officially*?" M.J. asked.

"I mean there's no housing here for the site manager or any of the rangers. We close the main gate at sundown and one of your marked cars makes sure there are no cars left in the parking lots. After that, everybody's supposed to be gone," he replied.

"Dodd, I know everyone is *supposed* to be gone, but is there anyone still here on a regular basis?" she asked with a note of irritation in her voice.

He looked up and said, "Yes there is. There's a homeless guy with a camp back in the forest. He's a Vietnam vet. Lives there with his dog. He doesn't bother anybody and we just leave him alone. He was a Navy corpsman attached to a Marine unit and he's administered first aid to some of the rangers when they've fallen and cut themselves, things like that. One time, he even set a broken arm until we could get the ranger to the hospital."

"So why didn't you just tell me that in the first place?" she asked.

"Look, M.J., you know it's against the law for anyone to have a permanent camp site in a national park. The only way we could get him out would be to call you guys and have him arrested and we didn't want to do that. We actually like the guy and check up on him now and then to make sure he's alright. Like I said, he's helped us out several times and he doesn't bother anybody. I hope you won't report this to anybody," Dodd said.

M.J. thought for a moment and said, "I'm not going to report it, but I want to talk to him. When can I do that?" she asked.

"I'll have one of the rangers go by tomorrow morning and tell him to expect you. His camp is behind a big rock outcropping off the Swamp Trail. Not many people go back that way. I think the name of the trail puts them off," Dodd said.

"I'll plan on going to see him tomorrow afternoon," she said. "There's one other thing. I run every morning. I've been running at Hains Point, but I'd like to start running here so I can see who comes and goes in the park. Is that a problem?" she asked.

"Not at all," he replied. "There are lots of runners here every day. The park opens at seven in the morning, but I'll give you a key for the gate so you can come earlier if you want. We've got locker rooms in this building and you can shower and change there."

"Sounds great, Dodd. By the way, what's the homeless guy's name?" she asked.

"His last name is Wonders. I don't know his first name. We just call him Doc. His dog's name is Lola," he replied.

M.J. stood and they shook hands. "Thanks for the tour," she said. "I'll see you tomorrow."

CHAPTER SIX

M.J. stopped on the way to her apartment and purchased several extra-large T-shirts, big enough to hide her gun belt. It had occurred to her that she might encounter the murderer while she was running in the park and she didn't want that to happen while she was unarmed. When she ran at Hains Point, she didn't wear her gun belt and her rough calculation was that it—together with the gun, extra magazines, handcuffs, and pepper spray canister—would weigh about six pounds. She spent some time rearranging the items on the belt to balance the weight for running, then put it on and ran in place to try it out. Not perfect, she thought, but she could handle it.

The next morning, she went to Anacostia Station. The message light on her phone was flashing. It was Zerk asking her to come by the lab, which she did after downing a cup of coffee and checking the duty roster.

Zerk was sitting in front of a computer monitor when she entered the lab. He motioned her over to a table where the two bicycles ridden by the boys were lying on their sides along with their two helmets, all marked with evidence tags.

"There weren't any usable prints on the helmets, just smudges," he said, "but I think I've got something else that might be helpful."

He pointed to the front wheel of one of the bikes. "If you look carefully, you'll notice that the spokes are depressed in this area," he said, moving his finger in an arc over the wheel. "I think the killer may have stepped on it going after the other boy. Come over here and take a look at this."

She followed him to the computer where he had been working. He typed in some information and a picture of the wheel appeared.

"This is the wheel with the depressed area," he said, typing on the keyboard, "and this is a picture of the wheel that I took using a lens with a very short focal length to enhance the image of the depression." M.J. looked at the picture, which clearly showed an impression about the size of a foot. "It's not really usable as a footprint because there's no detail," he said, "but I was able to do some experiments that may give you some information."

Zerk got up from the computer and walked back to the table where the bikes had been placed. He pointed to a wheel lying by itself on the corner of the table.

"I was able to measure the depth of the depression using some instruments I have here in the lab. I bought the exact same wheel at a bicycle shop and then started placing weights on the spokes until they reached the same depth. Based on that, I'd say the murderer weighed between 180 and 200 pounds and, based on the rough size of the depression, I'd say he wore a size 12 or 13 shoe," he explained.

"Zerk, that's amazing," M.J. said, noting the look of accomplishment on his face.

"Actually, I can give you one more piece of information," he quickly added. "There is a rough correlation between a person's shoe size and their height. That size shoe probably belongs to someone who is around six feet tall, give or take an inch."

"That narrows things down," M.J. said. "Thanks, Zerk. Let me know if you figure out anything else."

She went back to her desk, passing Jake on the way.

"I'm going back out to Great Falls Park to interview someone who might have some information," she said to

Jake. "Zerk gave me some great stuff and, after I talk to the Medical Examiner, I may need your help in interviewing some more people."

"I'm in the process of finishing up an assault investigation, but I should be finished by tomorrow. Just let me know," he said.

"I'll do that," she said. "Oh, and if you want to have pizza tomorrow night, I'll buy."

"Deal," he said.

She went back to her car and started the drive to Great Falls Park. She arrived at the Visitor Center carrying her gym bag and stuck her head into Dodd's office.

"Good morning," she said. "Am I OK to stop by and see Doc later today?"

"I had one of the guys stop by his camp this morning to let him know you'd be coming," Dodd replied. "Are you going running?" he asked, pointing to her gym bag.

"I plan to do that right now. I'll see him after I finish and clean up. Thanks for the locker, by the way," she said.

"No problem. Enjoy your run," he replied.

She changed into her running clothes and shoes, fastened the gun belt around her waist and pulled the T-shirt over it. There was a full-length mirror in the locker room and she stopped to see how she looked. "It makes me look fat," she said aloud, "but that's the price of law enforcement."

Outside the locker room, she did her stretches and then began running down the trail past the overlooks. There were several other runners, men and women, taking the same path. She cut across to the Old Carriage Road and picked up her pace. The packed gravel surface was good for running and she was able to achieve a speed nearly equal to her Hains Point runs. Her breathing was measured and the gun belt was proving not to be a real problem.

She ran about two miles to the end of the Old Carriage Road, did a high-stepping U-turn, and headed back toward the Visitor Center. She passed more than a dozen runners coming the other way. They were mostly twenty-somethings. Some were wearing earphones listening to God-knows-what, oblivious to the natural beauty around them. She thought she recognized a couple of faces from one of the marathons she had run. None of the runners had the look of a killer.

When she reached the parking lot at the Visitor Center, she jogged in place for a few minutes, did some stretches and checked the GPS-enabled watch that she wore when she ran. It registered 5.2 miles—about the same distance she usually ran at Hains Point—and a little over thirty-eight minutes; slower than her usual pace, but not too bad. The next time she would vary the run to include some uphill stretches, like the Ridge Trail and the trail at Difficult Run, she thought. It would increase her time, but it would be good strength training and let her see who might be on the back trails, away from the twenty-somethings.

She took a quick shower and changed back into the dark blue pantsuit that was her normal workday outfit. She unclipped her sidearm from the gun belt and attached the holster to the belt she used with the pantsuit. She did the same with the handcuffs, pepper spray, and extra magazines. Instead of her regular work shoes, however, she pulled on her hiking shoes.

She walked by Dodd McMillan's office again. He was gone, but she was told that he was outside the building talking to several rangers. M.J. went out the side door and waited until he was finished.

"I'll need some directions to get to Doc Wonders' camp," she said.

"I'll be glad to take you up there, if you like," Dodd offered.

"That's OK. I'd rather talk to him alone, if you don't mind," she said.

"I understand," he replied. "It shouldn't be too hard for you to find. Just go back up the Old Carriage Road. The sign for the Swamp Trail is on the right."

M.J. remembered seeing it on her morning run. "Then what?" she asked.

"Just follow the trail," he said. "There are footbridges over some small streams coming out of the hills. Right after the second one, you'll see a path to the right that goes up a steep hill and around a big outcropping of rock. Follow it to the plateau at the top and you'll be at Doc's camp. Like I said, he'll be expecting you."

"Thanks. I'll stop by when I get back," she said.

As she walked down the Old Carriage Road, she began to develop a picture in her mind of what Doc Wonders probably looked like: He was a Vietnam veteran, which meant that he was in his late fifties or early sixties. He probably suffered from PTSD and would have a wild stare in his eyes. She expected him to be wearing an old uniform or some type of camouflage clothing. He would probably be unshaven and might have a full beard.

She entered the Swamp Trail. It was very rough and passed through a lot of rocky areas that required some navigation for safe passage.   She reached the second footbridge after a few minutes of walking and looked up to her right where she saw the path. It had several cutbacks, but she still had to be careful of her footing. In some places the ground was still wet and slippery from the heavy rain and she had to plant the toes of her shoes to keep from sliding backwards.

The plateau at the top of the path was about fifty feet square and trailed off into underbrush and woods on three sides. In the middle of the clearing was a large tent with a front awning, under which there were two canvas chairs and a small table.

Doc Wonders came around the corner of the tent, walking with a noticeable limp, followed by his dog. Her mental picture of a semi-crazed Vietnam vet couldn't have been more wrong. He was about six feet tall, trim and fit, wearing khaki pants and a polo shirt. His hair was trimmed neatly and he was clean-shaven.

"Hi, I'm Doc Wonders," he said, extending his hand. "You must be the Park Police person they said would be stopping by."

"M.J. Powers," she said, shaking his hand.

"Well, this is Lola," he said, motioning toward his dog, which looked to be some sort of yellow Lab and hound mix with short light brown hair, a white diamond patch on her chest and long spindly legs. She was one of those dogs that didn't just wag her tail, she wagged her whole body as she came over to greet M.J. with a dog smile on her face.

"Hello, Lola," M.J. said as she reached down to scratch the dog behind its ears. When she stopped scratching, the dog sat down and looked up at her with expectant eyes. "OK," M.J. said as she knelt down to pet the dog's head and back. "That's all for now."

"I just made some coffee," Doc said. "It's not Starbucks, but it's not too bad. I only have powdered cream though."

"I'd love some," M.J. said, "and black is just fine."

Doc motioned to the two chairs in front of the tent and M.J. sat down. Lola came over and pressed against her leg.

"Let me know if she's bothering you," Doc said as he walked over to a Coleman stove where he picked up a coffee pot.

"She's not bothering me at all," M.J. replied, scratching behind Lola's ears. "I grew up around dogs."

There were two mugs on the small table and he filled both. "I drink mine black too," he said. "I just keep the cream stuff around in case anybody wants it."

"So how did you wind up living here?" M.J. asked, taking a sip of the coffee.

"Well," he replied, "I was living at my folks' place in western Pennsylvania and I had hitchhiked down to the Navy Medical Center in Bethesda for treatment of some wounds I got in Vietnam. I was hitching back and the truck driver let me out on the Capital Beltway at the exit for Georgetown Pike. I started walking this way figuring it would be a shortcut home. It was getting toward dark and when I reached the entrance to the park I thought I'd just spend the night here and start hitching again in the morning.

"To make a long story short, I liked the place so much that I went back to Pennsylvania and made arrangements to sell the house there. My folks had both passed away and it really didn't have much attraction for me. Then I bought this tent and some supplies and hitchhiked back about a week later. I've lived here ever since."

"Where did you find Lola?" M.J. asked.

"It's more like she found me," he said. "She wandered into camp here about two years ago. She was just a pup, not even a year old. I put up signs at the Visitor Center and down in the village, but nobody ever claimed her."

"Why did you name her Lola?" M.J. asked, taking another sip of coffee.

"You know that old song 'Whatever Lola Wants.' Well, it seemed to fit her," he said, looking at the dog, which was still pressed against M.J.'s leg.

M.J. smiled and patted Lola's head. "It does seem to fit," she said and asked, "How do the two of you get money for food and supplies?"

"I get a disability pension from the V.A. for this," he said, patting his right leg. "It's not much, but it's enough for most everything we need. The checks come to general delivery at the post office in the village. Lola and I hike up there, cash them and pick up any supplies we need. The vet in the village takes care of Lola for nothing. She even gives me flea and tick repellant to use on her in warm weather and shampoo to keep her clean," he said, pointing to a shelf outside the tent with several bottles and boxes on it.

"What do you do to pass the time?" M.J. asked.

"I read a lot," Doc replied. "The library in the village gave me a card and I load up on books whenever we go in to pick up supplies. Lola and I also hike around the park almost every day. We really enjoy that."

"What trails do you hike?" M.J. asked.

"Pretty much all of them," he replied.

"Do you ever see people here in the park at night?" M.J. asked.

"Oh sure," he said. "Usually hear them more than see them. You know, kids riding on the trails or running around. They don't come over on the Swamp Trail very much, but they use the Old Carriage Road and the Ridge Trail a lot, especially during warm weather."

"What about Difficult Run?" she asked.

"We can't hear people on that trail from here, but when it's warm we sometimes go there at night when most of the people have left and jump in one of the pools in the stream. That's where I give Lola a bath with that shampoo and wash myself up too," he said.

"Have you ever seen anybody or anything suspicious on Difficult Run or any of the other trails?" she asked.

"Not really," he replied. "Mostly just hikers, runners, people walking their dogs, that sort of thing. I guess you're asking me these questions because of those two boys that were killed over on Difficult Run."

"That's right," she replied. "I'd appreciate it if you'd keep an eye out for anybody that is acting suspiciously. We think the murderer is probably around six feet tall and weighs 180 to 200 pounds."

"Anything else you can tell me?" Doc asked.

"We don't have much else right now," she replied, "but I'll let you know if we get any new information. Obviously, you shouldn't approach anyone yourself. I'll be running here in the park every day and probably making some night visits too. If it's OK, I'd like to stop by from time to time and check in with you."

"Well, Lola and I always like to have visitors, so just stop by anytime. We might see you out on the trails too," he said.

"I'll look forward to it," she said, finishing her coffee. She stood up and shook Doc's hand, then turned to give Lola one more scratch behind the ears.

She went back to the Visitor Center and found Dodd.

"Any trouble finding Doc?" he asked.

"None at all," she replied. "He's going to watch for people coming into the park at night and I'll be visiting him to check on anything he might have seen. I'd appreciate it if your people would watch for anything suspicious too."

"I've already asked them to do just that," he said.

"Thanks, Dodd. I appreciate it," she said and left to drive back to Anacostia Station.

CHAPTER SEVEN

M.J. was early for her meeting with the Virginia State Medical Examiner. She had expected to just receive a written report, but his assistant had called and asked if she could stop by and meet with him to discuss the deaths of the two boys.

As she sat in the small waiting room, she thought to herself how similar it was to the waiting rooms in other doctors' offices. Well-worn copies of *People, Us, Scientific American* and some assorted car magazines lay on a coffee table in front of four upholstered chairs.

The difference, she thought, was that this was not like a normal doctor's office where people came for treatment of a cold, persistent headaches or broken bones. Here, people came to discuss just one thing and that was death—the how, the why and the clinical details of the end of life, which had usually occurred under tragic circumstances.

The door opened and a man in his mid-forties with curly black hair entered the waiting room. He was tall, perhaps six-one or two and had reading glasses strung around his neck with a cord.

"Hi, I'm Doctor Martin," he said. "Come on back to my office."

She followed him down a short corridor and entered a relatively small office with a large window that flooded the room with light.   The walls were decorated with two diplomas and several prints of Marc Chagall paintings.   In the corner was a full-size model of a human skeleton.

"I appreciate you coming by. I thought that it might help with your investigation if we could talk about the exact cause of death of these two boys," he said.

"Well, I assume they died of broken necks," M.J. said, adding, "I saw the bodies."

"You're correct in the broadest sense, Detective Powers, but the term 'broken neck' covers a lot of different things," he said, pulling two files to the center of his desk. "People's necks are broken all the time and in all different ways— automobile accidents, diving into shallow water, sports injuries. In this case, the death certificate will say something like 'acute trauma to the cervical spine and spinal cord,' which is not much different than what I would put on one for someone who had died from an impact injury, like a car crash. Here, of course, we are dealing with an intentionally inflicted injury and that demands a more detailed explanation than the one that will appear on the official record."

"Is there something that might help us identify the murderer?" M.J. asked.

"There may be, but first let me tell you what I know about breaking people's necks. I don't mean me personally, of course, just from a clinical perspective," he said, displaying a broad smile.

"First of all," he continued, "the term 'broken neck' usually denotes damage to the cervical vertebrae." He rose from his desk and walked to the model skeleton in the corner. "The cervical vertebrae are the first seven below the skull," he said, pointing to that region on the skeleton. "The first vertebra is actually attached to the skull and most neck injuries involve the second and possibly the third vertebrae. Of course the real damage doesn't occur from the injury to the bone, it occurs because of trauma to the spinal cord that is protected by the vertebrae. If any of the cervical vertebrae are damaged badly enough, it will result in spinal cord injury. That, in turn, can cause unconsciousness, paralysis or death."

"How easy is it to break another person's neck?" she asked.

"Well, it's not like in the movies," he replied. "I mean when you see Sylvester Stallone or Arnold Schwarzenegger casually walk up to someone and twist their neck, it's a bit of an exaggeration. That could only happen if the person's neck and shoulder muscles were completely relaxed, which would not be the case if someone was about to kill them. Those muscles are very powerful and they involuntarily tighten to protect the spinal cord from such injuries."

"Then how is it done?" she asked.

"Well, the technique that's taught in military hand-to-hand combat involves using one hand to push or pull the opponent's head back, like this, to loosen the neck muscles," he said, first placing the heal of his hand under his chin and pushing back, then placing it on his forehead and pulling back. "The other hand comes around the head and quickly twists with a downward motion. This, at the very least, produces trauma to the second and possibly the third vertebrae with varying degrees of injury to the spinal cord.

"I know a lot about this type of injury because the Army paid for my med school education and while I was on active duty to pay them back I was stationed at Fort Benning. We used to see injuries caused by that maneuver three or four times a month, either through training accidents or fights in local bars. Some of the victims left with a neck brace; some left in a body bag."

"So you think these boys may have been killed by someone with military training?" she asked.

"Well, the killer may have been in the military at some point, but he didn't use the hand-to-hand technique I just described. The injuries these boys suffered were caused by someone turning their heads laterally against the full strength of their muscles. Given the age and physical condition of the boys, that would have been difficult and would have required considerable strength," he said.

"But their heads were turned completely around. Wouldn't that have required even more strength?" she asked.

"Actually, strength would only be a factor in initially breaking their necks. Once there was damage to the spinal cord, all muscle control would cease and turning the head farther would be relatively easy—like wringing the neck of a chicken," he replied.

M.J. remembered the time, as a little girl, she had surreptitiously watched her grandmother fetch a chicken for dinner. She had picked the chicken up by its neck, swung it up in the air and then brought it down with a quick circular snapping motion. The chicken's head was turned completely around. *Like the boys' heads*, she thought.

"I x-rayed both of the boys' necks before I started the autopsies. Their injuries were almost identical. The second and third vertebrae weren't just fractured, they were completely dislocated. Here, you can see it quite clearly," he said, holding up an x-ray film.

"These injuries are similar to what is usually referred to as a 'hangman's fracture.' It gets its name from the type of damage that occurs in executions by hanging where the head is forcibly pulled up by the noose under the chin and the full weight of the body causes the vertebrae to be pulled apart. In the case of these boys, however, this separation of the vertebrae was accompanied by a violent rotation of the head which literally shredded the spinal cord in both cases.

"I called in a colleague who is an orthopedic surgeon to take a look. He concurred that this could only have been done by a sharp, continuous lateral twisting motion. Neither of us had ever seen anything like it," he said, adding, "These boys died as close to an instant death as is medically possible."

She pondered this for a moment, then asked, "So would it be correct to say that we're looking for someone with considerable upper body strength?"

"Yes, and probably someone at least six feet tall to allow a direct approach to someone seated on a bicycle," he said. "The killer must have attacked from behind and pulled the boys' heads back, probably with the aid of their helmets, judging from the bruising where the helmets struck the base of their skulls. The subsequent rotation of their heads was in a clockwise direction, so the killer was most likely right-handed."

"But why, after killing the boys, would the person continue turning their heads around?" M.J. asked.

"I don't have an answer for that question, Detective. It is, you might say, a bit of overkill," he said.

"Thanks, Doctor. This has been very helpful. May I give you a call if I have any more questions?" she asked.

"Absolutely," he replied, rising from behind his desk and glancing down at one of the folders, "and there's one other piece of information. Based on the readings taken by your technician at the scene and the condition of the bodies when we got them, I'd estimate the time of death at between 8:00 and 10:00 p.m. Sunday night."

He walked with her back to the waiting room. As she turned to leave, she asked, "By the way, why did you pick this particular medical specialty?"

He thought for a moment, then replied, "Well, it's intellectually challenging, the hours are good," he paused, then smiled and added, "and the patients never complain."

CHAPTER EIGHT

M.J. met Jake at their favorite pizza place near the waterfront in Old Town Alexandria. They each ordered a beer while they were waiting for the pizza. M.J. tossed the Metro section of the *Washington Post* on the table.

"Did you see this?" she asked.

"Not yet," Jake replied, thumbing through the paper. On page four was a small article with the headline *MURDERS IN GREAT FALLS PARK*:

> *The bodies of two McLean residents were found early Monday morning in Great Falls Park. Police are investigating the deaths as homicides. The victims were Steven Marsten and Patrick Hager, both age 17, of McLean. A spokesman for the U.S. Park Police declined to elaborate on the case, except to say that the victims appear to have*

been trail biking in the park late Sunday
night when the murders occurred.

"It'll probably be in the community papers when they come out tomorrow," M.J. said. "I met with the Medical Examiner this morning. He said that the killer had to have a lot of upper body strength to do this. Zerk did some tests and said we're looking for somebody around six feet, 180 to 200 pounds. The M.E. also said the person is probably right-handed."

"That's not much to go on," Jake said.

"No shit," she said, "but it's all we've got for now. I'm thinking about canvassing the gyms in the metro area to see if anything turns up."

"What good would that do?" Jake asked. "You've seen the people at our gym. At least half of them do workouts to develop upper body strength. Short of finding somebody practicing breaking the necks of mannequins, I doubt that there'd be any good leads."

"What about ex-military?" she asked.

"Same thing," he replied. "There are a lot of active duty and former military people in this area and a lot of them work out at gyms. Besides, if somebody wanted to work out with murder in mind, they could always buy some gym equipment and work out in the privacy of their home."

"That's true," she said, taking another drink of beer. "Well, I made appointments to interview the parents and some people at the boys' school tomorrow. I hope you can come along for those."

"I finished the case I was working on today, so that shouldn't be a problem," he replied. "What about the person you were going to interview at the park?" he asked.

"He's a homeless guy who has a campsite and I asked him to keep an eye out. Don't say anything about him to Swain. The rangers like him and don't want him kicked out. Besides, he's the best set of eyes we've got in the park at night," she said.

"Are you planning to keep running there?" he asked.

"Yep, and probably make a few nighttime visits too," she said, "although from what I've seen so far most of the people on the trails are pretty harmless looking."

"Did you check the National Crimes Database?" Jake asked.

"Yeah," she replied. "The closest things are murders by hanging. There are no reported homicides involving violently broken necks."

"By the way, I called our guy assigned to the Joint Terrorism Task Force," Jake said. "I remembered that the hijackers who crashed the plane into the Pentagon had been working out at a gym in suburban Maryland for several months before 9-11. They were building their upper body strength so they could overpower the crew and passengers. I thought our case might be a practice run for another terrorist attack."

"What did he say?" M.J. asked.

"He shopped it around at the JTTF. The consensus was that because the bodies were left it doesn't fit with the profile for terrorists," Jake replied. "They go out of their way to stay below the radar screen. He couldn't completely rule out a terrorist connection but thought it was pretty unlikely."

The pizza came and they each took a piece. They ate quietly for a few minutes, then M.J. said, "This case is driving me nuts. You know the drill for analyzing homicides: means, motive, opportunity. Problem is, we only have one, the means, for sure. The only part of opportunity in the equation was being in the right place at the right time. As for motive, I'll be damned if I can figure one out short of pure psychopathic behavior."

"Well, the way in which they were killed certainly points to a psychopath, but that doesn't give us much of a solid lead," Jake said.

"I know," she said. "What we really need is some luck."

They finished the pizza together with a second beer. As they left, M.J. spotted a pet store across the street and pulled Jake after her.

"Why are we going to a pet store?" he asked.

"Need to get something for a friend of mine," M.J. replied, entering the shop and picking out a bag of high-end dog treats. She paid for them and they went back out onto the street.

It was a beautiful spring evening, warm with the scent of blooming trees imprinted on the breeze from the river. As they walked back toward their cars, Jake asked, "Why don't you come over to my place?"

"I think I'll pass tonight," M.J. said. "I'm really wound up with this case and I also need a good night's sleep."

When they got to the parking lot, she put her arms around Jake's neck and gave him a lingering kiss. "See you in the morning. Our interviews start at 11:00," she said as she started to walk to her car.

Jake took her arm and gently pulled her back. He kissed her and said, "You know things would really be a lot simpler if we just lived together."

"I know," M.J. replied. "I'll seriously think about it. Maybe when this case is wrapped up we can do something."

Jake smiled and said, "The way this case is going, that's a pretty open proposition."

On the drive to her apartment, M.J. decided that living with Jake wasn't such a bad idea. After all, they had maintained an exclusive relationship for almost two years and sharing an apartment with him wasn't such a big step. She also realized that her continued resistance to the idea might threaten their relationship and she didn't want that to happen.

When she entered her apartment, she took off her gun belt and clothes and fell into bed. She was asleep in minutes.

CHAPTER NINE

M.J. arrived at Great Falls Park just after sunrise the next morning. She changed into her running clothes and started down the Old Carriage Road. She turned onto the Swamp Trail, which required that she slow her pace to avoid the rocks and fallen tree limbs. When she reached the path to Doc Wonders' camp, she climbed halfway up and then called out to make sure that he was there.

"Doc, it's Detective Powers. OK if I come up?"

"Sure is," he called back. "You're just in time for coffee."

Lola appeared at the top of the path, wagging all over. M.J. patted her head and said, "C'mon girl. I've got something for you."

Doc was sitting under the tent awning and there were two cups of coffee on the little table. M.J. reached into her pocket and took out one of the dog treats she had purchased the night before. "Sit," she said and Lola obediently sat down, her body wiggling in anticipation. M.J. gave her the treat and the dog looked up at her expectantly.

"Do you want another one?" M.J. asked.

Lola responded with her dog smile and tried to control her excitement. M.J. gave her a second treat and walked toward the tent with the dog following closely behind her.

"You're spoiling her, you know," Doc said, handing M.J. her cup of coffee.

"I know," said M.J., "but I couldn't come empty-handed."

M.J. sat down and took a sip of coffee. "I was out running and thought I'd stop by," she said.

"Glad you did," Doc said. "I've been thinking about what you asked when you first stopped by—about whether I'd seen anything unusual at night. Don't know why I didn't remember it before, but about a year ago I did see something that seemed pretty odd."

"What was that?" M.J. asked.

"Well, it was early spring. I know that because the leaves weren't on the trees yet. It had been raining hard for a couple of days, lots of thunder and lightning to boot. Lola and I had just stayed holed up in the tent. Only went out for necessities. The storm started to taper off the second night and I came out here under the flap to check things out. I was looking toward the ridge over there when there was a big flash of lightning. That's when I saw a guy moving through the trees on the ridge," he said. "I remember thinking it was pretty strange for anybody to be out in weather like that."

"What did he look like?" M.J. asked.

"I can't give you much of a detailed description," he said. "I only saw him for an instant when the lightning flashed. Also, he was pretty far away. I'd have to say that he was pretty big, though. He was kind of hunched over, but I'd guess he was around six feet tall.   Pretty hefty in the shoulders, but I couldn't see much detail. It looked like he was wearing a jacket or sweatshirt or something like that with a hood pulled up over up his head. When the lightning flashed again, he was gone."

"Could you tell if he was black or white?" M.J. asked.

"I remember seeing his face sticking out from the hood and it looked white," Doc replied.

"Which way was he heading?" M.J. asked.

Doc pointed to the south. "That way," he said, "toward Difficult Run."

"Anything else?" she asked.

"Nope. But if I remember something, I'll sure let you know Detective," he replied.

"Call me M.J., please," she said.

"OK, M.J.," he said. "By the way, if you want you can take Lola along on your run. She doesn't get to run very much. I mean we go for lots of walks, but with this gimpy leg of mine, running isn't on the agenda."

M.J. looked down at Lola, who was pressed against her leg, and asked, "What do you think, girl? Does that sound like a good idea?"

The dog jumped up and began barking and turning in circles.

"You can take that as a 'yes,'" Doc said, smiling. "There's a leash right over there."

M.J. and Lola started running when they got back to the Old Carriage Road. M.J. started slowly and the dog kept her pace, looking back occasionally as if to seek approval. As M.J. increased her stride, Lola matched it, never straying from her right side.

They ran about three miles and circled back to Doc's campsite. When they reached the tent, M.J. reached into her pocket, took out another treat and gave it to the dog. "Good girl," she said, scratching behind Lola's ears.

Doc was sitting where they had left him, sipping his coffee. "How'd she do?" he asked.

"Great," M.J. replied. "A born runner."

"Feel free to take her along anytime," he said.

"I'll do that," M.J. said. "I plan on running every day, but it may not always be at the same time. Is that a problem?"

"As you've probably noticed," Doc said, smiling, "we don't have much of a schedule, so just stop by when you're in the neighborhood."

"Will do," M.J. replied, giving Lola one more scratch behind the ears. "By the way, thanks for the information on what you saw last spring. It may be very helpful."

"No problem," he said.

"I've got to go now, but I'll probably see you tomorrow," M.J. said, turning toward the trail.

When she got back to the Visitor Center locker room, she showered and changed into her pantsuit. Jake was going to pick her up so they could go to the interviews in McLean, but she had a few minutes and stopped by Dodd's office.

"M.J.," he said, looking up from his desk. "How are things going?"

"Fine," she said. "Have any of your people seen or heard anything?"

"Nothing," he replied.   "A couple of reporters came around yesterday, but we told them any questions had to be referred to your office."

"Thanks for that," M.J. said.   "We're holding back any details on the murders for the time being."

"Understood," he said.   "I'll let you know right away if we come up with anything."

"Thanks," she said.   "See you in a couple of days."

She walked out to the parking lot where Jake was waiting in his unmarked car.

M.J. had interviewed a lot of families of victims. Sometimes it produced useful information; usually it did not. She was not looking forward to meeting with the boys' parents because it was likely to only be an encounter with the raw edge of grief and little else.   But it was one of the items on the checklist of an investigation, and it had to be done.

The Marsten residence was on a quiet, tree-lined street in McLean.   Compared to some of the sprawling homes in the area, it was quite modest.   The car they had found in the parking lot at Difficult Run was tucked to one side of the driveway, the bike rack still attached to its bumper.

They rang the doorbell and were met by David Marsten, a tall man with graying hair, probably in his late forties.

"Please, come in," he said. "My wife and the Hagers are in the living room."

As they entered the room, the three parents rose from their seats. The two mothers were wearing black knee-length dresses. The fathers were dressed in suits and ties. All of them had the haggard look brought on by unbearable grief.

One of the women stepped forward and held out her hand. "I'm Jean Marsten, Steve's mother," she said. "This is Phil and Kate Hager, Patrick's parents."

M.J. and Jake shook everyone's hand and sat down in two chairs opposite a sofa and a loveseat where the parents were sitting.

"We apologize for bothering you during this difficult time," M.J. said, "but there are a few questions we need to ask to help us find whoever murdered your boys."

"Anything we can do to help . . . anything," Phil Hager said.

"What can you tell us about your boys and why they happened to be in Great Falls Park the night they were killed?" M.J. asked.

David Marsten was the first to speak. "Steve and Patrick were fast friends since kindergarten. They played together when they were little, were on the lacrosse team in middle and high school, went on dates together—you could say they were inseparable. They were already making plans to apply to the same colleges," he said.

Kate Hager had taken out a piece of tissue and was dabbing at her tears. "They loved adventure, particularly extreme sports," she said. "They went bungee jumping in West Virginia, did all kinds of acrobatics on their skate boards—you know, half pipes, that sort of thing—and they were very much into trail biking. They were always going to Great Falls Park and had ridden in Shenandoah and some of the other national parks. About four months ago, one of them read in a biking magazine about a new adventure sport that involved riding trails at night. They went out and bought lights for their helmets and started practicing after dark in the parks here in McLean. We think they had been to Great Falls Park at night before, but we're not sure. They weren't supposed to go anywhere without telling us, but you know how that is with teenagers. They were good about not going out on school nights though, and we think the only reason they were in Great Falls Park the night they were killed was that the next day was a school holiday."

Phil Hager interrupted. "How in the hell were they murdered, Detective? When Dave and I went to identify the bodies, they kept the sheets tucked up under the boys' chins to hide their necks. Now the mortuary is telling us that if we want open caskets, they'll have to dress them in turtlenecks to hide the bruises," he said.

"Their necks were broken," M.J. said matter-of-factly. "If it's any comfort, the Medical Examiner said they both died instantly."

"You mean someone broke their necks?" Jean Marsten gasped, putting her fingers to her lips.

"Yes," M.J. replied. "We are keeping that information very close, however, while we're conducting the investigation and I would ask that you not share it with anyone."

"Who would do such a thing?" Jean Marsten asked.

"That's what we're trying to figure out Mrs. Marsten," M.J. said. "Anything any of you might know about anyone who would want to kill the boys would be very helpful to us."

"How many people do you think were involved?" David Marsten asked.

"We don't know for sure," M.J. replied. "Based on what evidence we have, it appears that the same assailant killed both boys, but that doesn't mean there weren't others involved."

"I can't imagine anyone wanting to kill our boys, can you?" Kate Hager asked, turning to look at the other parents, all of whom shook their heads in agreement. She added, "I mean they were popular at school, didn't do any drugs, and played sports . . ."

"Was either of them dating anyone?" Jake asked.

"Patrick had been dating the same girl since Middle School," Kate Hager said, turning to look at Jean Marsten. "Jean, hadn't Steve just started dating someone new about a month ago?" she asked.

"That's right," Jean Marsten replied. "A nice girl. I'll give you her name if you like," she said, turning toward Jake.

"We'll actually need both girls' names," Jake said. "We may want to talk to them."

Jean Marsten took a pen and paper from the coffee table, wrote down the girls' names and handed it to Jake. "They both go to Langley High School, same as the boys," she said.

"When are the boys' funerals?" M.J. asked.

"This Friday. There's going to be one service for both of them and they'll be buried next to each other . . . We thought they'd want it that way," Phil Hager replied, his voice cracking and tears forming in his eyes.

"We want to thank all of you and offer our deepest condolences," M.J. said, rising from her chair and handing each of the parents one of her cards. "If you think of anything that might help us, please call me. My cell phone is on the card and I'm available 24/7."

"Thank you Detective, and please let us know if you find out who murdered our boys," David Marsten said. They all shook hands and he lead them to the door.

Jake and M.J. drove to a deli in McLean to grab something to eat before their next appointment.

"That wasn't very helpful," Jake said.

"No, it wasn't, but I didn't expect it to be," M.J. replied. "Frankly, I don't think we'll get much usable information at the school either, but we still have to try."

They ordered sandwiches and drinks. While they were eating, M.J. told Jake about her conversation with Doc.

"Well, that physical description seems to fit with what we know," Jake said.

"Yeah, and someone out in a thunderstorm creeping through the woods at night sounds pretty psychopathic too," M.J. offered.

"Still not much to go on," Jake added as they finished eating and headed to the car.

"You've got that right," M.J. said. "Let's see what we can find out at the school."

Langley High School is a sprawling complex on the outskirts of McLean. When M.J. and Jake arrived they immediately noticed a large black ribbon that had been carefully tied around a giant boulder at the entrance to the parking lot. The base of the rock was piled high with bouquets of flowers. Hundreds of notes and cards had been taped to the stone face.

Jake parked the car and they entered the school through its front entrance. They checked in at the front desk and were escorted to the principal's office.

Students were milling about in the corridor, removing books from lockers and talking quietly to friends before going to their next class. M.J. noticed the somber expressions on most of their faces and the black armbands that many of them were wearing. She remembered how she had felt in high school when two of her friends had died in an automobile accident and the collective grief that had consumed student life for weeks thereafter. This, she thought, has to be much worse because the boys were murdered.

They entered the office and were met by a man in a polo shirt and slacks. "I'm Paul Chambers, the principal. We'll be meeting in here," he said, motioning to a conference room.

There were two other men standing next to the table when they entered.

"This is Randy Keating, my assistant principal and Tony Lambert, who coaches our lacrosse team," Principal Chambers said.

They all shook hands, introduced themselves and sat down. M.J. started the conversation.

"As you know, we are investigating the murders of Steven Marsten and Patrick Hager. We wanted to ask you a few questions and would be interested in anything you might know that would help us," she said.

"We all knew the boys," Principal Chambers began. "They were both good students and never got in any trouble here at school."

"They were both first string on the varsity team from day one," Coach Lambert added. "Really good players. We won the Virginia State Championship twice with them on the team. Frankly, I don't know how we'll be able to replace them for this season."

"Ever any fights between either of the boys and other students?" Jake asked.

"None," Assistant Principal Keating said. "If there had been, I would have known about it. School discipline is part of my responsibility. Coach, anything ever happen between them and the other players?"

"Oh, hell no," Coach Lambert replied. "They were very popular with the other guys. They were co-captains of the team this year and last. The only time I ever saw them get rough with anybody was against opposing players during a game, and that's just part of the sport."

"Any drug problems that you're aware of?" M.J. asked.

"None," said Keating. "Of course we have drug problems here; most every school does. But these boys didn't run with that crowd."

"The parents gave us the names of the boys' girl friends," Jake said, sliding the piece of paper across the table. "We're thinking about interviewing them to see if they might know anything."

"I thought you might. I already checked and neither of them is here today," said Keating. "They're upset, I'm sure.

A lot of the kids are. We've had to bring in grief counselors from several other schools to help deal with this. I doubt the girls will come back to school until after spring break, which is next week. I can send you their home addresses and phone numbers if you want to reach them there."

"We'd appreciate that," M.J. said. "Is there anything else any of you can think of that might help us?"

The three men looked at each other and shook their heads.

"I guess we'd like some information from you, if possible, Detective," said Principal Chambers. "Can you tell us anything about how the boys were murdered? There hasn't been much in the papers."

"That's intentional," M.J. replied. "We're holding back a lot of information while we conduct our investigation. The only thing I'm able to tell you right now is that the boys suffered trauma to their necks and I'd appreciate it if that went no further."

"Of course," Principal Chambers replied. "We'll certainly get in touch with you if we hear anything that might be useful."

M.J. and Jake shook the men's hands and M.J. gave them her card. Principal Chambers walked them back to the front entrance. "Thanks for all you're doing," he said when they reached the doors.

Jake drove M.J. back to her car in Great Falls Park. As she was getting out, she asked, "Got any plans tonight?"

"None. What did you have in mind? A movie and dinner?" he asked with a smile on his face.

"A late dinner, but instead of a movie I'd like to go for a nice walk," she replied.

"A walk? Where?" he asked.

"Difficult Run. I'll pick you up at your place at eight sharp," she said.

CHAPTER TEN

M.J. picked Jake up at eight, as promised. They were both wearing casual clothes and windbreakers to hide their gun belts. It was an unusually warm night for early April; so warm that under other circumstances they might have skipped the windbreakers.

The parking lot for Difficult Run was filled with cars. At first, M.J. wondered about this until she remembered that it was spring break for a lot of the colleges in the area. She suspected that Difficult Run was a popular place to gather and party.

Her suspicions were confirmed when they entered the trail and could hear music and voices. When they rounded the first curve, they saw a large gathering of college-age kids around a bonfire that had been built in a hollow surrounded by high rock walls. To the right, they could hear the sounds of splashing water and uncontrolled laughter and giggling.

"Well, Detective," Jake said as they walked past the area, "we seem to have several violations of the law going on here. An open fire and the consumption of alcoholic beverages in a national park . . . and I wonder just what is going on down in the stream. I think I should investigate."

"Bullshit, Jake. You *know* what's going on down there. You're just looking for the chance to see some naked college girls," M.J. said.

"You know, there are probably naked college *boys* too," Jake replied.

"Hmmm . . . tempting, but we're here for other things. If you feel really strongly about it though, we can call it into Fairfax County on our way out.   Let them be the party poopers," M.J. said.

"You're no fun," Jake said. "By the way, just what *are* we here for?"

"Just keep walking and let me think," M.J. replied.

Jake knew M.J. well enough to know that meant to shut up. They kept walking, using the small flashlights from their gun belts to illuminate the trail in front of them. There was a quarter moon that provided some illumination in the areas without overhanging trees, but it was generally dark enough to require close attention to the path in front of them. M.J. had been down the trail several times in daylight but not at night. Jake had not been back since the murder investigation started.

After several hundred yards, the sounds from the party died out and the only thing that could be heard was the rushing water in the stream below. A bird with a wingspan of several feet swooped out of a tree and came gliding down the trail just above head level. Jake started when the bird flew over, ducking and instinctively reaching for his gun.

"What the hell was that?" Jake exclaimed.

"Just an owl looking for food," M.J. replied nonchalantly, continuing on the trail in silence.

They reached the point where the murders had occurred and M.J. stopped, shining her flashlight around the surrounding rocks. She stood there for several minutes, lost in thought.

"Let's go back to the car," she said.

A few yards up the trail, she turned to Jake and said, "There was only one killer."

"How do you know that?" he asked.

"Think about it," she said, "he would have come here at night. Probably parked in the lot where we did. He was looking to murder someone, anyone. There were probably people up at the head of the trail, just like there are tonight. That seems to be a very popular place. If there had been more than one killer, they would likely have murdered someone there. Maybe waited until a lot of the people had left, then killed the stragglers. One of them could have blocked the escape route while the other committed the murders.

"I also have a hard time believing that two psychopaths would join up for an evening stroll on this trail in search of victims. For one thing, it doesn't fit the pattern for that type of killer. They usually work alone. That's part of the thrill for them. Also, there's the way the boys were killed. If it was more than one person, the method of choice would have been guns so they could do more damage."

"Maybe one liked to do the actual killing while the other just liked to watch," Jake replied.

"Can't rule that out," M.J. said. "We're dealing with some really dark corners of the human mind. But if there was more than one killer, the gathering place up there would still have been more attractive. After all, they couldn't be sure there was anyone else on the trail that night.

"A lone killer would have bypassed the party. Too little opportunity; too many witnesses. He would have walked on down the trail, maybe looking for a better victim, maybe just out of frustration. When the boys' helmet lights appeared at the top of the Ridge Trail, it presented the perfect opportunity. The killer would have had plenty of time to hide. He would figure out that if he killed the first boy and kept the second from riding back up the trail, there would be no witnesses. After that, he could just walk back to the parking lot and leave the way he came."

"Wouldn't somebody at the party have seen him arriving or leaving?" Jake asked.

"Maybe, but we just walked by there and no one saw us. I'll bet they don't see us when we leave either," M.J. said.

As predicted, they walked past the hollow without being noticed. When they got back to the car M.J. said, "It just occurred to me that if there were people partying there that night, the boys may have known some of them. Hard to say if they would have stopped to say hello. If there was drinking going on, they probably wouldn't have. It's probably worth putting up some posters at Langley and the other schools in the area asking if anyone has any information, though. We can put the TipLine number on the posters and see if anything shakes out."

"I'll take care of that tomorrow," Jake said.

They stopped on the way to Jake's apartment and picked up some Chinese take-out and a bottle of wine. Jake opened the wine and poured each of them a glass, raising his in a toast.

"Here's to a great date. Let's do that again real soon," he said sarcastically. "By the way, why didn't you spook when that owl flew over?"

"You're such a city boy, Jake," she replied. "I grew up in the hills of West Virginia. We had owls fly over our heads all the time."

They finished eating and while they were rinsing off their plates, Jake asked, "How about spending the night?"

M.J. turned toward him, gave him a kiss, and said, "Yes, I think I'd like that very much."

CHAPTER ELEVEN

M.J. stopped by her apartment early the next morning. She showered and changed into her pantsuit, then drove to Anacostia Station where she wrote an interim report on the investigation, carefully omitting any mention of Doc Wonders. She handed it to Detective Sergeant Tony Lauretta.

Tony had spent ten years in the Marine Corps. He had a wife and two children who he saw very little of as a Marine, so he decided it was time for a career change and joined the Park Police. Tony was about five feet eight inches tall with extremely close-cropped hair and built as solidly as anyone M.J. had ever seen. Although he tried to present a gruff manor, he was actually very kind and considerate in dealing with the people who reported to him.

"Glad you're turning this in, M.J. The Lieutenant has been bugging the hell out of me about whether there's been any progress in the case," he said.

"I'll try and give you updates so he'll stay off your back," M.J. said. "By the way, sorry I've been missing so many roll calls. I'm spending a lot of time at Great Falls Park on the investigation."

"That's OK, M.J.," he replied. "I'll let you know if anything important comes up."

"Thanks, Tony," M.J. said and left for the park.

She changed into her running clothes and headed for Doc's campsite. When she reached the bottom of the path, Lola appeared at the top with her leash in her mouth, wagging all over. M.J. went up the path and found Doc sitting under the tent awning in his usual chair.

"Did you teach her to do that?" M.J. asked, pointing to the dog.

Doc raised his open right hand and said, "Honest, she figured it out herself, M.J. You know, 'whatever Lola wants.' How about a cup of coffee?"

"Sure, I'll have a quick one. Seen or heard anything of interest lately?" M.J. asked.

"Not a damn thing," Doc replied. "How's your investigation coming?"

"Slowly," she replied. "We've interviewed several people but haven't gotten any leads so far. It's early though, so maybe we'll get a lucky break."

"Well, I'll keep my eyes and ears open," he said.

M.J. finished her coffee and picked up the leash, which Lola had conveniently placed at her feet. "C'mon girl. Let's do our run," she said.

They ran the Old Carriage Road to the Ridge Trail, then over the top of the hill to Difficult Run. As they started up Difficult Run, M.J. was struck by the difference in the atmosphere of the place in daylight compared to the night before. In the dark, it had seemed closed in, almost tunnel-like. Now, it was truly beautiful, she thought, with trees in bud and the sound of the stream below punctuated by birds excitedly calling to each other. For so early in the day, there were a considerable number of people on the trail. Mostly hikers and dog walkers; not many runners.

They crossed Georgetown Pike and started back on the Old Carriage Road. When they reached Doc's camp, M.J. scratched behind Lola's ears and gave her a treat. She held out the leash and the dog took it, ran to the front of the tent, dropped it and came back for a second treat, looking up at M.J. with wide eyes and a smile. "OK," M.J. said, "I'll give you another one this time, but only because you did such a good job of keeping up."

Doc came around the corner of the tent and said with a smile, "You're really spoiling my dog, M.J."

"I know," she replied. "See you next time."

The next morning, she parked unobtrusively outside the church where the boys' funeral was being held and watched the arrival of the mourners. She knew that killers sometimes attended the funerals of their victims for reasons that she found hard to fathom.

The parking lot filled up quickly and the Fairfax County Police started directing traffic to an alternate lot where a shuttle bus had been hastily called into service. By her rough count, around a thousand people came to the funeral, most of them kids from Langley, many of them crying and leaning on each other for support. She watched until they had all either entered the main sanctuary or been diverted to an attached fellowship hall with a closed-circuit television hook-up. She knew this showing of love and support would help the parents of the boys and she felt a twinge of guilt for being there to spy on the crowd. It was, however, part of her job. Unfortunately, she didn't see anyone who even remotely raised her suspicions.

She continued to run almost every day in the park, both because she enjoyed running and because it was a good way to watch the comings and goings there. She ran at different times of the day and on different trails to make sure she was observing the totality of the park visitors. She also went back to Difficult Run several times at night to observe the activity there.

After several weeks, she knew many of the regulars on the trails, some of whom said "hello" when they saw her. For the most part, the consistent park visitors were either young runners, hikers, people walking their dogs or older people just taking a leisurely walk. There were also the daily visits to Mather Gorge by kayakers and rock climbers.

Before starting her daytime runs, M.J. always stopped by Doc's camp. She rationalized this in her own mind as being the same as checking in with an informant when doing undercover work, but she knew that she had actually developed a degree of affection for Doc and, of course, Lola, who she always took along on her runs. On several occasions, she had even given them both a ride into town so Doc could pick up his mail and supplies and return library books.

Jake had distributed the TipLine posters to the schools in the area and the case had been added to the Most Wanted List on the Park Police web site. So far, neither had produced any information.

In early May, she and Jake were assigned as backup for a raid by the Narcotics and Vice Unit in the notorious Trinidad section of the District of Columbia. They donned bullet-proof vests and pulled in behind the "jump-outs", a slang term used by residents for the unmarked cars carrying plainclothes narcotics officers. Their main function was to handcuff and guard some of the dozen or so people arrested until the van arrived to take them to jail.

During the week before Memorial Day, they, along with all uniformed and plainclothes Park Police, were assigned to security on the National Mall and at Arlington National Cemetery for the ceremonies and other events.

Even with these duties and the assignment of other criminal investigations, M.J. was able to go to Great Falls Park every day. She failed to see anyone suspicious, but she kept running and watching.

CHAPTER TWELVE

M.J. went running with Lola on the Tuesday morning after Memorial Day and repeated the routine on Wednesday. She still didn't see anyone suspicious on the trails.

By Wednesday night, she was tired, troubled and frustrated, and she wanted to go home for a few days. She decided she would leave on Friday afternoon and be in Ronceverte in time for her mother's home-cooked dinner. That was just what she needed; that and the chance to sit on the front porch and talk to her father about the case.

On Thursday morning, she went to Tony Lauretta and said, "I'd like to take tomorrow afternoon off."

He looked up from some papers he was reading and said, "Why don't you just take the whole day off, M.J.? You've got lots of leave time and there's not much going on right now."

"Afternoon will do," she said. "I may want to use the half day another time."

Tony said, "OK. Enjoy your time off."

When she got back to her desk, she picked up her cell phone and scrolled to the number marked "Home," pushed the send button and waited.   Three rings later her father answered.

"I've heard great things about your bed and breakfast," she said.   "Got room for a guest tomorrow around dinner time?"

"I think we do, but I'll need to let the kitchen know which of our featured specials you'll be having. I checked the menu and I believe they are fried chicken and meatloaf," her father replied.

"Hmmm. I think the fried chicken sounds perfect," M.J. said.

Her father laughed and said, "I'll let the cook know. Can't wait to see you, Honey."

"Love you Dad. Mom too. See you tomorrow," M.J. said.

She drove her personal car, a four-year-old midnight blue Ford Mustang, to Anacostia Station the next morning and cleaned up some pending paperwork.   At noon, she said goodbye to Jake and headed home to see her parents.

It was about four and a half hours to Ronceverte, a small town tucked into a valley in the Appalachians in West

Virginia. Most of the drive would be on Interstates, with the last few miles on a two-lane road that snaked through the mountains. It was a beautiful, cloudless day and she was enjoying the power and handling of her Mustang.

She crossed the Shenandoah River about an hour after leaving Anacostia and got her first glimpse of the Blue Ridge Mountains. She immediately felt herself start to relax, thinking less about work and more about where she was headed.

Her parents, Walt and Ginny Powers, were in their early sixties. Walt was not her birth father, who had been killed in a head-on with a drunk driver out on U.S. 219 when she was six months old. He had supported her and her mother working in the management office of one of the coal mines. After he died, her mother took a job as a waitress in the coffee shop at the Greenbrier Resort in White Sulphur Springs, which was about thirty minutes away from Ronceverte. On the days that her mother was working, M.J.'s maternal grandmother, who lived about a mile down the road, took care of her.

As part of her duties in the coffee shop, her mother took care of a room off the kitchen where breakfast and lunch were served to visiting tradesmen and law enforcement officers. One day at breakfast, she saw a tall West Virginia state trooper at the table. Her mother always said that she fell in love with Walt the minute she set eyes on him. Walt would always smile and say that he just liked her because she served such great breakfasts.

They got married about a year later and Walt legally adopted M.J., whose given name was Martha Jean, although she had insisted on being referred to by her initials since age six. When she was in second grade, Walt transferred to the State Police Bureau of Criminal Investigation. She remembered asking him why he didn't wear the trooper hat that she liked anymore and didn't drive the car with the flashing lights on the top. Her father had told her that he still had the hat, but his new job required that he dress like other folks and drive a regular car so the bad guys couldn't figure out who he was. She liked that.

She had always been a runner. In grade school, she would challenge the boys to footraces, which she usually won. Her middle school had a cross-country team that she joined without hesitation and in high school her team competed in all of the state and regional meets, where M.J. always finished in the top three slots. During her senior year, the cross-country coach from West Virginia University in

Morgantown stopped by the house to ask if she would be interested in going to school there and joining the team. With the encouragement of her parents, she applied and was accepted.

She majored in criminology and applied herself to her studies while spending all of her spare time training and competing in cross-country. Her team was consistently ranked nationally in the top ten by the NCAA and she won several personal awards during her junior and senior years.

She tried to get home to Ronceverte whenever she could, but her schedule made that difficult, except for holidays. However, her father seemed to find reasons to regularly visit Morgantown on "official business" and they would always have lunch or dinner together. She would tell him about case studies in her criminology courses and he would tell her as much as he could about investigations he was handling. They loved each other's company and loved talking shop.

During her senior year, they would often talk about what she wanted to do after college. Law enforcement, of course, but where and what was the question. He discouraged her from joining a state or local agency. "Too much bullshit stuff," he would say. She thought about the FBI, but it required two years of job experience before applying and she didn't want to wait that long. Then, one day, there was a job fair at the university for majors in criminology and forensics. She went and looked at the materials from several federal police agencies.

She stopped at the desk for the United States Park Police. She didn't know much about it, except the horse-mounted police she had seen on her high school field trip to Washington. The brochure said they were the oldest police force in the United States and covered all of the national monuments and parks. She was interested and filled out an application form. About a week later, she received a phone call asking if she could come to Washington and take an exam and a physical fitness test. She went and passed both.

She called her father to ask what he thought about her joining the Park Police. In typical fashion, he said, "I don't know much about them, but they're cops, right? If it seems right for you, go ahead with it. If nothing else, you'll get some training and experience. If you don't like it, you can always use that to transfer to another federal agency."

After she graduated from college, she went back to Washington for an interview with a panel of Park Police officers. She was told that she had been accepted and, after being sworn in, attended a one-week orientation in

Washington before transferring to the Federal Law Enforcement Training Center in Glynco, Georgia. After eighteen weeks there, she came back to D.C. for more training. Her parents came to her graduation ceremony and her father, while trying to appear stoically unaffected, wound up having to dab some tears from his eyes.

That was almost six years ago. Since then, she had done foot patrol duty on the National Mall, cruiser patrols on the GW and participated in all of the security details manned by the Park Police. She took the detective exam after three years on the force and, after passing it, was transferred to the Criminal Investigations Branch as an investigator.   Two years later, she was made a detective.

M.J. left the Interstate and began the drive through the mountains toward Ronceverte. There were occasional small houses, many with yards littered with automobiles, trucks and boats resting on cinder blocks, anxiously awaiting repairs that would probably never come. At some of the junctions, there were small convenience stores with ancient gas pumps out front. This was the West Virginia landscape that she had known as a child and it had changed very little. In some ways, it was comforting to know that it still existed in sharp contrast to the urban existence that now defined her world.

She turned up the gravel road that led to her parent's house, a white 1920s bungalow with three second-floor dormers and an open porch across the entire front. Her parents were sitting on the porch and came down the steps when she pulled up. Her father, a towering figure at six feet four inches, came forward and wrapped his arms around her.

"About time you got here," he said, releasing his hug so that M.J. could embrace her mother. "Don't you pay him any mind," her mother said, "we're just glad you got here safely."

M.J. retrieved her suitcase from the back seat of her car and the three of them walked up to the house. The living room had a pleasant and familiar smell that evoked a jumble of memories for M.J. Her mother was shorter than she was and had graying hair cut to shoulder length. She plucked an apron from one of the chairs, put it on and said, "You just freshen up and go sit with your father on the porch while I start dinner."

M.J. walked up the narrow stairs to the second floor and took her bag into her bedroom, which was virtually unchanged from her high school days. The corner bookcase held all of her cross-country trophies and medals, and there were two posters still attached to the walls, one for the 1996 Summer Olympics in Atlanta and another for the rock group

Nirvana. She smiled as she looked around the room and touched the comforter on her bed, which had been made by her grandmother when M.J. was still in grade school.

She splashed some water on her face, took a file folder out of the side pocket of her suitcase and headed for the porch.

Her father was sitting in one of the two rocking chairs and had placed an open beer for each of them on the table in between. M.J. handed him the file folder.

"This is a case I need to talk to you about," she said.

He opened the folder and looked at the crime scene picture of the two boys' bodies. It took a moment for the reality to register, much as it had for M.J. that morning at Difficult Run.

"M.J., this is horrendous!" he exclaimed. "For God's sake don't let your mother see this!"

He paged through the file, reading M.J.'s reports of the Medical Examiner's findings, Zerk's forensic investigation, and the interviews she and Jake had conducted. When he finished, she told him about the figure Doc had seen a year before and the daily runs she was doing to look for a suspect.

"Honey," he said, "I've seen a lot of murder scenes and people killed in a lot of ways, but nothing like this. I investigated a couple of lynchings in the southern part of the state, but that's the closest thing to these boys' murders."

"Dad, it's frustrating me that there are no leads," she said.

He thought for a moment then said, "Well, I guess you've already figured out that the crucial thing here is the way they were murdered. That tells a lot about the person you're looking for. I don't think you're going to find a motive. This was somebody really sick and you may see their work in the future, but then again you may not. I think you're right to run in the park. You run every day anyway, and that's the best place to spot the killer."

"Thanks, Dad," she said.

Her mother appeared at the door and said, "Dinner's ready if you two sleuths are finished."

As they got up to go inside her father handed the file back to her and said, "Now you go put that away before we eat."

The fried chicken was as good—actually better—than M.J. remembered. She heaped mashed potatoes and fresh corn on her plate to go with it.

"Honey, have you been eating enough?" her mother asked, watching her devour the meal and take a second helping.

"Yeah, Mom. I just don't get food this good," she replied.

They talked about happenings in Ronceverte and her mother seemed to provide a lot of information about M.J.'s classmates who had gotten married, were pregnant or already had children. M.J. knew this was a thinly-disguised suggestion that she should be considering the same thing.

"How is your friend Jake?" her father interjected. M.J. had brought him home one weekend to meet her parents.

"He's OK," she said. "We're still dating and of course we work together."

"He seems like a very nice boy," her mother said.

"He is," M.J. responded and tried to change the subject. "Are a lot more people out of work here?" she asked.

"It sure looks that way," her father replied. "Of course, there's not as many people living here as there used to be. I know some of the stores downtown are having a real tough time."

They ate in silence for a while. M.J. was stuffed, but her mother started clearing the table and said, "I made a fresh apple pie and you father picked up some ice cream. Want some?"

"Sure," M.J. said, knowing that it would push her over the edge. It was only seven o'clock and she was already feeling sleepy.

M.J. got up early the next morning and put on her running clothes. She headed up the steep hill behind her parents' house, the same hill she had run as a child. There was a trail along the ridge that lead to the town of Ronceverte and she increased her pace. She missed having Lola running next to her but did not miss the added weight of her gun belt.

She came down off the ridge and followed the trail to Main Street, passing Rudy's Corner Grill where she had worked as a waitress on weekends in high school. The town only had a population of 1,500 and M.J. knew most of its residents. She passed several people who waved and yelled out her name or "Good to have you back!" She had run this same route every day growing up and she enjoyed the familiarity.

She cut over to Edgar Avenue, which ran parallel to the railroad tracks. A long freight train hauling coal was moving slowly through the town and M.J. instinctively tried to outrace it, just as she used to do as a girl.

At the end of town, she cut back to the trail along the ridge and then along it to her parents' house. When she arrived, her father was sitting on the front porch with a cup of coffee. She gave him a kiss on the forehead and sat down.

"How have you been feeling, Dad?" she asked. "You look like you've put on a little weight. Are you getting enough exercise?"

"I actually feel pretty good," he said. "Since I retired I probably haven't been getting as much exercise as I should, but I walk into town once or twice a week. It's your mother's cooking that's made me put on some weight."

M.J. smiled. "Just because she cooks it doesn't mean you have to eat it all," she said.

"I know, I know," he replied, patting his stomach.

M.J. gave him another kiss and went to the kitchen where her mother was cooking bacon and eggs. She hugged her and poured some coffee for herself.

"Mom, don't cook a lot of that for me. I'm not much of a breakfast eater," she said.

"Whatever you don't eat, I'm sure your father will be glad to finish," she replied cheerfully.

"I know," M.J. said, "but he needs to cut back on his eating and get some exercise, too. I just told him so."

"That's what I tell him all the time, but it doesn't seem to make any difference," her mother replied.

"Speaking of which, how have you been feeling, Mom?" M.J. asked.

"Oh, I really feel fine," her mother replied. "My legs get a little achy sometimes, but that's from all the years I spent on my feet waitressing. Other than that, no complaints."

M.J. stepped back and looked at her mother. "Well, you look great, Mom," she said.

"Aren't you sweet," her mother said and gave her a hug. "Now go tell your father it's time to eat."

Over breakfast, M.J. told them about the people she had seen on her run.

"You were such a fixture with your daily runs I'll bet some of them thought they were in a time warp," her father said, laughing.

"Why don't you and I go downtown a little later and do some shopping," her mother said to M.J.

"That would be great," M.J. replied. "Dad, I brought a couple of movies for us to watch this afternoon, if you're up for it."

"You know me. I'm always up for a movie," he said, dishing the last of the scrambled eggs onto his plate.

That evening, M.J.'s mother made meatloaf. It was delicious and M.J. once again ate enough to make her sleepy.

She was only able to join in a game of Scrabble until about nine o'clock. "I'm going to have to leave you two to duke it out. I need to get going fairly early tomorrow," she said.

"That's OK, Honey," her mother said. "I think you probably can use the sleep anyway."

M.J. got up the next morning and had coffee on the porch with her parents. Her father carried her bag out to her car.

"I know that case you're working on is frustrating as hell," he said, "but trust your instincts and you'll be OK. Yours have always been good and that's what will help you solve it."

She gave him a hug. "Thanks, Dad," she said.

CHAPTER THIRTEEN

M.J. was still frustrated with the lack of progress in the murder cases, but the weekend with her parents had helped to put things more in perspective. She found herself lessening the intensity, if not the frequency, of her surveillance of people in the park.

There seemed little else that she could do but wait for a break of some sort. Thus far, none of the public appeals for information had produced anything at all. The parents of the murdered boys had called M.J. several times to see if any progress had been made in the investigation. In early June, David Marsten called to say that the families and some friends had put together a reward of $10,000 for information leading to the arrest of the killer or killers. M.J. explained that it would be difficult to obtain any federal reward money, but that she would try. In the interim, she said, the families' offer would be added to the public information on the case. A small article about the reward appeared in the Metro section of the *Washington Post* and similar stories were published in the community newspapers.

It was now mid-June, more than two months since the murders had occurred, and still nothing. M.J. continued to run in the park every day and to walk Difficult Run at night.

She was beginning to wonder if her daily runs had a chance of producing any usable information when she saw something that caught her attention. It was late in the day and she was just getting ready to turn off the Old Carriage Road onto the Swamp Trail to pick up Lola when she saw a solitary figure running ahead of her. He was about six feet tall with a shaven head and massive shoulders and biceps that stretched the material of his gray T-shirt to the limit. He was wearing running shorts and M.J. could see that he was in very good shape. She decided to follow him.

He was running, not jogging, but M.J. still had to slow her usual pace so she didn't overtake him. She stayed back about a hundred yards to keep from being noticed, but he never looked behind him.

At the Ridge Trail, he started up the steep slope without noticeably reducing his speed. M.J. followed, still keeping her distance. He disappeared over the hill on the trail, and she slowed to make sure she didn't accidentally catch up to him.

When she reached the crest of the hill, he had almost reached the bottom of the trail where it intersected with Difficult Run. M.J. was about to start running again, when he suddenly stopped at the juncture of the trails. She stopped and stepped behind a tree.

He was near the spot where the boys had been murdered. He slowly surveyed the area from right to left but never looked in the direction where M.J. was hiding.   Then something strange happened. He bowed his head and his huge shoulders began to shake. It took M.J. a moment to realize that he was sobbing.

He suddenly fell to his knees, still sobbing, and placed his face in his hands. He stayed that way for several minutes until he finally stood up, using the sleeve of the T-shirt to wipe his eyes. He started moving up Difficult Run, not running this time, but walking slowly, his head still bent.

M.J. made her way carefully down the Ridge Trail and waited until he was once again about a hundred yards ahead of her position. He was still walking and she did the same. There were a few other people on Difficult Run and she noticed that when he passed them he straightened himself and seemed to be avoiding any kind of eye contact.

He kept walking until he reached the parking lot, where he went over to a late model Dodge Charger, opened the door and got in. M.J. went to a car directly opposite, placed her foot on its bumper and pretended to be doing stretches while she memorized his North Carolina license plate number.

After the car left the parking lot, M.J. called Jake on her cell phone and gave him the plate information.

CHAPTER FOURTEEN

By the time M.J. got to Anacostia Station, Jake had run the license number and had left a copy of the report on her desk. She briefly looked at it and walked over to his desk.

"So what gives?" he asked.

She explained how she had followed the man in the park, his physical description, and his strange actions near the murder scene. Jake nodded his head and said, "Definitely sounds like something worth pursuing."

The plate had come back as registered to a Franklin C. Cody with an address in Jacksonville, North Carolina, a town just outside Camp Lejeune. The plate had not been registered with any of the local jurisdictions, but M.J. found a matching telephone listing in Springfield, Virginia. She waited a hour and called it. A man answered the phone.

"Is this Mr. Cody?" M.J. asked.

"Yes, this is Sergeant Cody. What can I do for you?" he replied.

"Sergeant, this is Detective Powers of the United States Park Police. I was wondering if we might set up a time to meet and ask you a few questions."

"What kind of questions?" he asked.

"Well, we're conducting an investigation and we thought you might be able to help us," she said.

"I don't understand. Am I in some kind of trouble?" he asked.

"No, Sergeant. We would just like to meet and ask you some questions. It's completely voluntary on your part, but we would really appreciate it," M.J. said.

"Where is it you want to meet?" he asked.

"We're located in the Park Police station in Anacostia Park. Do you know where that is?" she asked.

"Yeah, sure. I've gone running there a few times," he said.

"Is there sometime tomorrow that might work for you?" M.J. asked.

"Well, I'm temporarily assigned to the Marine Corps Barracks which is just across the river from you. I could come by when I get off duty at four," he said.

"That would be great. We'll look for you around four thirty, if that's OK," M.J. said.

"Sure, I'll see you then. By the way, do I need to bring a lawyer or anything?" he asked.

"You can if you want, but we just want to ask you some questions," M.J. responded.

"OK, I'll be there," he replied.

M.J. turned to Jake, who had been listening on the other line. "This should be interesting," she said.

Sergeant Cody arrived promptly at four thirty, without an attorney, and was escorted to the conference room on the first floor where M.J. and Jake were waiting. He looked to be in his late twenties or early thirties, but his eyes had a vacant stare that made him appear much older. He was wearing the Marine Corps uniform consisting of a short-sleeve khaki shirt and drab green trousers. His hat was tucked tightly under his arm.

His shoulders and arms were as massive as M.J. remembered from the trail, and his chest, which she had not seen, was equally well developed. She surmised that he had to have his shirts tailored to fit his physique.

His shirt was adorned with three rows of medals and M.J. recognized a Silver Star and what she thought was a Bronze Star. He towered over both her and Jake.

"Please have a seat Sergeant," she said. "Thank you for coming."

"Yes Ma'am. What is this about?" he asked.

"Well, as I said on the phone, we just want to ask you a few questions," she replied. "I guess the first question is whether you have you ever been to Great Falls Park?"

"Yes Ma'am, yesterday, as a matter of fact," he replied.

"Is that the first time you'd been there?" she asked.

"Yes Ma'am," he replied.

"And why did you go there?" she asked.

"A friend of mine told me it was a good place to run, so I thought I'd try it out," he responded.

"You ran down a trail to a place called Difficult Run and stopped and looked around. Why did you do that?" M.J. asked.

"How do you know that?" he asked.

"I was behind you on the trail," M.J. responded.

"What's wrong with stopping and looking around?" he asked.

"Nothing. But then you started to cry, sob really," M.J. said.

"I don't know what you're talking about," he said with some irritation.

"Sergeant, I was right behind you on the trail and I saw you start crying and then fall to your knees with your face in your hands," M.J. said.

"I still don't know what you're talking about," he said. "Why are you asking me these questions anyway?"

"OK, Sergeant. There were two murders committed very near the place where I saw you stop and start sobbing and we'd like to know what you know about them," M.J. said. "Just tell us why you stopped there and started crying."

Cody looked down at the floor. He seemed to be composing himself. When he looked up he asked, "Are you going to tell my C.O. about this?"

"Not based on anything we've heard so far," M.J. replied.

Cody hesitated and took a deep breath. "Three years ago," he said, looking at the floor again, "a squad I was leading was ambushed by the Taliban on a trail by a stream in eastern Afghanistan. The place looked just like the place where I stopped when I was running yesterday. Three of my men were killed in that ambush and two more seriously wounded. I guess when I saw that place in the park I had some kind of a flashback. It just came out of nowhere and completely overwhelmed me. I've had some other problems like this, but they didn't bring me down this hard."

M.J. gave him a few moments before speaking.

"One last question Sergeant, she said. "Where were you on April 4 of this year?"

"That's easy to answer Ma'am," he replied. "I was in Helmand Province in Afghanistan with the 2nd Battalion of the 8th Marines."

M.J. and Jake looked at each other in stunned silence.

When she finally spoke, M.J. said "Thank you for meeting with us." She hesitated and then said, "And thank you for your service."

After Cody had left, M.J. turned to Jake and said, "I need a drink."

CHAPTER FIFTEEN

She went running the next morning. As usual, Lola was ready with her leash and Doc was ready with a cup of coffee.

"How are things going?" Doc asked.

"OK, I guess," M.J. replied. "Thought I had a good suspect yesterday, a guy that matched the description we're looking for and was acting strangely. It turned out to be a Marine with PTSD and an iron-clad alibi—he was in Afghanistan when the murders occurred."

"Well, I know about Marines and I know about PTSD," Doc said. "Those kids fighting in these wars now, they're all coming back with PTSD, not to mention those that come back with limbs missing, their brains scrambled . . . or their bodies come back in a box. At least now they know what PTSD is and hopefully they can treat it. Didn't know anything about it when I came back from Vietnam; didn't even give it a name."

"Did you have PTSD Doc?" she asked.

"Oh, sure," he replied. "I was a Navy corpsman assigned to a Marine unit. It would've been hard not to have it. Problem is, none of us knew what it was and didn't understand what the effects were. It took all of us a long time to realize that a lot of the things we were feeling and doing were caused by it. A lot of guys from that era still suffer from the effects and still don't even know it. I was lucky. While I was hospitalized, I got the chance to talk to other vets and we kind of did some informal group therapy. If it hadn't been for that, I would have been more screwed up than I am. I still drank too much for twenty years, but I realized one day that that was no way to live so I started going to AA meetings and haven't had a drink since. Of course"—he laughed—"I *am* living in the woods with a dog.

"But enough about all that. Is this Marine doing OK?" he asked.

"Well, I hope so," M.J. replied. "He's having flashbacks and drew my attention out there on the trail because he completely broke down and started sobbing."

"I'll bet he wanted to make sure you wouldn't tell his commanding officer about it, didn't he?" Doc asked.

"Actually, he did," she said. "What was that about?"

"Real simple, M.J. Marines don't cry, or at least they don't want anybody to know that they do. It's part of the creed," Doc explained.

"Well, I feel sorry for him," she said. "Hell, I feel bad about even questioning him, but that's my job."

"Don't worry about it, M.J. It had to be done," Doc said.

She and Lola left on their run and came back about an hour later.

"I may not see you guys for a few days," M.J. said when they returned. "We're coming up on the Fourth of July and I imagine I'll pull some duty down on the Mall."

"Well, we'll see you whenever. Be careful," Doc said.

M.J. scratched Lola behind the ears and, at the dog's insistence, gave her another treat.

She drove back to Anacostia Station where the assignments for the Fourth of July were just being posted. As she anticipated, she and Jake had been assigned to security on the National Mall beginning the next day and continuing through the following Monday, the Fourth.

They dressed like tourists and spent a lot of time sitting on benches watching for suspicious characters. By the weekend, the Mall was already filling up with people and by

Monday the crowd was estimated at well over six hundred thousand. By the time the fireworks display ended and the crowds had dispersed, it was approaching midnight. They were both exhausted.

They picked up a bottle of wine and some take-out at a late-night deli and went back to M.J.'s apartment. After they ate, they both collapsed on her bed and fell sound asleep.

CHAPTER SIXTEEN

M.J. got to Anacostia Station at about 7:00 a.m. with the idea of finishing some paper work before she went to Great Falls Park. Around 8:30 a.m., her phone rang. It was Dispatch. A call had come in on the TipLine at 8:27 a.m..

M.J. went to the communications room and asked one of the dispatchers to play the recorded message. It was a man with no discernible accent:

> *If you want to know about the boys'*
> *killing, look to the Bible and read*
> *Deuteronomy 21:1-8.*

There was nothing else. M.J. had the dispatcher make a CD of the recording. Although they didn't advertise it, the TipLine also had caller ID and she wrote down the number.

She figured there weren't many Bibles in the building, so she went back to her desk and looked up the passage online. There were several different versions, but the English

Standard translation appeared under the heading "Atonement for Unsolved Murders":

> *If in the land that the LORD your God is giving you to possess someone is found slain, lying in the open country, and it is not known who killed him, then your elders and your judges shall come out, and they shall measure the distance to the surrounding cities. And the elders of the city that is nearest to the slain man shall take a heifer that has never been worked and that has not pulled in a yoke. And the elders of that city shall bring the heifer down to a valley with running water, which is neither plowed nor sown, and shall break the heifer's neck there in the valley. Then the priests, the sons of Levi, shall come forward, for the LORD your God has chosen them to minister to him and to bless in the name of the LORD, and by their word every dispute and every assault shall be*

settled. And all the elders of that city nearest to the slain man shall wash their hands over the heifer whose neck was broken in the valley, and they shall testify, 'Our hands did not shed this blood, nor did our eyes see it shed. Accept atonement, O LORD, for your people Israel, whom you have redeemed, and do not set the guilt of innocent blood in the midst of your people Israel, so that their blood guilt be atoned for.'

Creepy, she thought, but the phrase *bring the heifer down to a valley with running water . . . and . . . break the heifer's neck there in the valley* certainly caught her attention. It sounded a lot like Difficult Run, not to mention the reference to neck breaking.

She did a reverse number lookup from the caller ID. It came back as a pay phone at a convenience store in Sterling, Virginia. She went to her car and started driving.

The voice on the TipLine could be that of the killer, she thought, and the biblical reference could be the motive she had been looking for. Perhaps this was a psychopath who felt his actions were directed by God. Worse yet, it could be some kind of religious cult that performed ritual killings. Of course, it could also just be some religious nut.

The pay phone at the convenience store was outside and there was no security camera in view. There was one inside, however, and she persuaded the manager to let her replay the tape from earlier that morning. She watched the customers from thirty minutes before the call until thirty minutes after. There were lots of Hispanic landscape workers, a few harried commuters grabbing coffee or cigarettes, but no one who came even close to the description of the killer. She asked the two clerks who had been behind the counter during that time period if they had seen anyone acting strangely, particularly a tall person with bulging muscles. They said they had been very busy during that time but didn't remember anyone like that.

M.J. went back to her car. She looked at the biblical quotation again: . . . *someone is found slain . . . and it is not known who killed him.* In other words, she thought, an unsolved murder. She took out her cell phone and called Fairfax County Police Headquarters. She was put through to Ted Sommers, a detective she had worked with in the past.

"Hello, Ted, this is M.J. Powers from the Park Police. Are you going to be around long enough for me to stop by, say in thirty minutes?" she asked.

"No sweat, M.J.," he said. "See you when you get here."

She drove to the Judicial Center in Fairfax and parked outside Police Headquarters. Ted met her in the lobby. He was short with a smiling face and wore his hair in a badly designed comb-over to hide his baldness. He was also developing a paunch, probably from sitting at his desk or riding in cars all day.

"C'mon, I'll buy you a cup of coffee," he said, and led her across a courtyard to a cafeteria. They went through the line and then sat down at a table near a window.

"So what's up?" he asked. "I haven't seen you since we worked that assault case, maybe a year ago."

"Well, I'm working on the investigation involving the murder of those two boys in Great Falls Park," she said.

"How's that coming?" he asked.

"Slowly, very slowly," she replied, "but we got an anonymous call on our TipLine this morning from a guy who said we should look at a passage in the Bible. I checked it out and it refers to atoning for unsolved murders. Thing that's interesting, though, is that the passage refers to a scene that's really similar to the location of the murders and also refers to the way the boys were killed. We've been withholding that information and it struck me as worth following up. How many unsolved murders do you guys have, anyway?"

"Recent history, probably 30; ancient history, another 70 or so," he said. "By the way, we obviously withhold information in cases too, but it's surprising how fast a lot of it becomes public knowledge. I think it's the Internet and all the social networks that are popping up. I'd be willing to bet there's stuff on Facebook about your case."

"I haven't checked, but you're probably right," M.J. said. "What I'm looking for is an unsolved murder that might qualify for retribution."

"You know, the stuff about a biblical passage rings a bell," he said. "Let's go back to the office and talk to Dee Jessee. She works a lot of homicide cases and I remember her saying something about some information like that coming in on our tip line."

Dee was sitting at her desk and Ted pulled over two chairs after introducing her to M.J., who briefed her on the call.

"Let me guess," Dee said, "the message started with 'If you want to know about the murders, look to the Bible and read this passage.'"

"Pretty close," M.J. said.

"Sounds like the same guy we hear from all the time. Did the call come from a pay phone in Sterling?" Dee asked.

"Sure did," M.J. replied.

"Yeah, probably the same guy," Dee said. "He calls in the same message with different biblical references on most of our homicide cases, although he also seems to chime in on deviant sexual behavior too. We got one reference to the Book of Romans involving a guy who was flashing his privates to young boys. The passage said something about 'pederasty' and I had to look that one up."

"What the hell does that mean?" Ted asked.

"It means sex between men and boys," Dee replied with a mischievous smile on her face.

Ted grimaced.

"So, do you have any idea who this guy is?" M.J. asked.

"We think he's a retired minister with a lot of time on his hands," Dee said. "He lives in Sterling, not far from the pay phone. We thought about going after him for filing false police reports but decided that's pretty hard to do when all he's making us do is read the Bible."

"Yeah, I could see where that might be a problem," M.J. said, laughing. "But thanks for the information. You just saved me a lot of time."

CHAPTER SEVENTEEN

October passed without incident. There were no more suspicious runners; no more TipLine calls. The parents of the murdered boys continued to call about once a month to see if there had been any progress in the case. Each time, M.J. had to tell them that there had not been any progress, and each time she felt an added burden to solve the case as quickly as possible.

M.J. and Lola ran through the autumn forest in Great Falls Park each day surrounded by the now brilliant colors of the trees. By the beginning of November, the trails were covered with leaves that produced a tiny whirlwind with each stride.

She and Jake had Thanksgiving brunch with some friends at a restaurant that served the traditional meal "family style," another way of saying "more than you can possibly eat." M.J. had the server box her share of the leftovers and took them to Doc that afternoon.

In early December, there was a storm that left about two inches of powder snow on the ground. She and Lola were undeterred in their running, although M.J. swapped her T-shirt for an oversized sweatshirt.   The number of people visiting the park had dropped sharply, with only the regulars appearing on a daily basis.   Because of the snow and the resulting ice, everyone stuck to the flat trails. The sections of the River Tail along Mather Gorge were closed as being too dangerous.

One morning, while she was having coffee with Doc before her run, M.J. said, "I'm going home to West Virginia for Christmas.   Why don't you and Lola come along? There's plenty of room and I know my parents would love to meet you."

"That's really sweet of you to ask, M.J.," Doc said, "but you know Christmas is the only day the park is closed all year and we kind of like having it all to ourselves.   The rangers have a little party on Christmas Eve and they always invite us, so that's really our holiday celebration.   Besides, you need to spend that time by yourself with your folks."

Jake was going to spend Christmas with his parents and sister in upstate New York. He and M.J. exchanged gifts over dinner two days before Christmas.   M.J. had bought him several DVDs of recently released movies and he gave her a sterling silver bracelet. They watched one of the DVDs and went to bed early since both had to travel the next day.

"I'd rather be spending Christmas with you, you know," Jake said as they left the next morning. M.J. kissed him and said, "Maybe next year," adding, "Somewhere warm would be nice."

She had bought and wrapped a cable-knit sweater for Doc and a giant rawhide bone for Lola and took them by the camp on her way to West Virginia. "Still wish you'd come with me, but I understand your reasons for staying," she said.

"You just have a wonderful Christmas with your folks and we'll see you when you get back," Doc replied.

On the way to Ronceverte, M.J. could see that the Blue Ridge Mountains were already snow-covered and the Appalachians to the west appeared to have an even heavier coat. As her car climbed through the mountains on the back roads, it began to snow and by the time she reached her parents' house it was coming down in large, wet flakes.

When she pulled up at their house, her father came down to take her bags. "Looks like you made it just in time," he said. "They're predicting a couple of feet at least."

They went inside where a bright, crackling fire was burning in the fireplace. M.J. asked her father to leave the two large bags of presents by the decorated tree and sat down in one of the chairs in front of the fire.

Her mother came in and gave her a hug. "You just relax, Honey. I'm making some chili and corn bread for our Christmas Eve dinner and we can eat whenever you want," she said.

M.J. looked out the window at the snow, which was now falling quite heavily. Her father came downstairs from putting her bag in her room, went in the kitchen and came back with two beers.

"So how you doing M.J.?" he asked.

"Pretty well Dad," she replied. "Still working on the case we talked about and still frustrated by it."

She told him about the encounter with the Marine and the TipLine call.

"Dead ends are kind of par for the course with any investigation," he said, taking a drink of beer. "Patience is always a virtue, particularly in homicide cases. Trust me, I've had firsthand experience."

"I know, but it's still frustrating," she said.

"Is your Lieutenant bugging you about it?" her father asked.

"Oh yeah. He asks my Sergeant about it almost every week. I think he'd like to hand it off to the FBI and get rid of the case so it's not on his record," she replied.

"Well, you keep your claws in it and don't let him pressure you. There's nothing the Bureau can do that you haven't already done," he said.

Her mother came in and sat down in the other chair. "Are you two finished talking police stuff?" she asked.

"Pretty much," her father said, looking at M.J.

"Yeah, Mom," M.J. said.

"Well, we can eat whenever you're ready," M.J.'s mother said.

"Now would be a good time," her father said, taking a last drink from his beer.

They ate at the kitchen table, a family tradition on Christmas Eve, and exchanged a lot of small talk about happenings in Ronceverte. M.J. helped her mother clear the table and wash the dishes.

"Everything going OK with you?" her mother asked as she was putting the last plate in the drying rack.

"Pretty well I guess," M.J. replied.

"How about your social life?" her mother asked. "Are you and Jake still dating?"

"We're still dating, but that's about it for my social life. There's just not much time left for anything else," M.J. said.

"Do you think you two might get married some day?" her mother asked.

"Well, Jake thinks we should, but I'm not sure I'm ready to make that kind of commitment yet," M.J. replied. "We're thinking about living together, though. How would you feel about that, Mom?"

"Well, when I was young they called that 'shacking up,' but things have changed, I'm sure. After all, M.J., you're twenty-eight years old and you don't need approval from me or your father for anything you do. We just want you to be happy, that's all," she said.

"How do you think Dad would feel about me living with Jake?" M.J. asked.

"In truth, he probably wouldn't like the idea," her mother replied, "but I'll take care of that. You just do what's right for you. By the way, do you love Jake?"

"I think so Mom, but we're different in so many ways that it scares me," M.J. replied.

"Honey, you have always been independent, and I mean since you were a little girl. I doubt that you'll find anybody that's not different, but that's not such a bad thing," her mother said. "Your father and I are certainly different, but I think that's what has made our marriage work. Who would want to be married to someone who agreed with everything they said or did?"

"I suppose you're right Mom," M.J. replied. "Maybe I can focus more on that once I get past this murder case I'm working on." She turned and hugged her mother.

They went back into the living room and sat down in front of the fire with M.J.'s father.

"So, are you going to leave milk and cookies out for Santa?" he asked.

"I was thinking more along the lines of a Bloody Mary and some mixed nuts," M.J. replied with a smile.

"Santa approves," he said.

"OK," she said, "but if you try to wake me up really early, all bets are off."

When M.J. got up the next morning, her mother was already in the kitchen cooking. M.J. grabbed a cup of coffee, then put some mixed nuts in a bowl and made a Bloody Mary for her father.

"Here you go, Santa," M.J. said, placing the drink and the nuts on a table next to her father, who had just come downstairs.

"Ho, ho, ho," he said, taking a sip of the drink. "You have been a very good girl and Santa will make sure you get lots of nice presents."

Her mother came in after a few minutes and said, "Well, everything is cooking. Why don't we open our presents."

M.J. had gotten her father a wool mackinaw and her mother a fancy cookbook stand together with a newly-released edition of *Joy of Cooking*. Her mother had knit her a matching blue stocking cap and scarf. "Now you wear those when you're running so you don't catch cold," she said.

Her father gave her a pair of Thinsulate gloves. "You can still draw your gun when you're wearing them," he said. "I checked it out in the dressing room at the store with my gun."

Her mother scowled. "What a nice Christmas thought for your daughter!" she said.

After a relaxed Christmas meal of fresh turkey and her mother's homemade stuffing and side dishes, they sat around the fire making small talk. Her father nodded off a few times and M.J. came close to doing the same. The three of them did the dishes together and then M.J. and her father used a walk-behind snow blower to clear the driveway out to the main road, which had already been cleared by the county crew.

The next day was a federal holiday and M.J. didn't leave until late morning. Her father carried her bag out to her car and gave her a hug.

"That case you're working on," he said, "just remember the words of the great Sherlock Holmes . . .

M.J. rolled her eyes. Here it came—another Sherlock Holmes quote. She had given him a two-volume set of the complete Sir Arthur Conan Doyle series for Christmas a few years ago. He had sat down in front of the fireplace and read them both nonstop. Since then, he would periodically use quotes to punctuate his conversation.

" . . . *When you have eliminated the impossible, whatever remains, however improbable, must be the truth.*"

She smiled. "Thanks, Dad," she said.

CHAPTER EIGHTEEN

The morning after she came back from Ronceverte, M.J. checked in at the Anacostia Station and then headed to Great Falls Park. The sky was overcast and there was a gusting wind from the northeast that made the wind chill well below freezing.

She stopped by Dodd's office before changing into her running clothes. He was earnestly studying some graphs and printouts on his desk.

"Hi, Dodd," she said. "Did you have a good holiday?"

"I did indeed," he said, looking up from his desk. "My daughter and her boyfriend came out from Wyoming for Christmas and announced that they're getting married. How was your holiday?"

"That's great news about your daughter!" M.J. said. "I went home to West Virginia and had a very nice time."

"Much snow over there?" he asked.

"Oh yeah," she replied. "Lots up in the mountains and we got a good two feet while I was there."

"I've been looking at the National Weather Service long range forecast," Dodd said. "They're saying we're going to have a lot of snow this winter, particularly in the higher elevations. What worries me is what happens in the spring. If it gets real warm early, the snow will melt all at once and we'll have flooding down here for sure. Not much I can do about it, I guess. Just like to be prepared."

"Probably a good idea to be worried *and* prepared, Dodd. I'll check in with you on the case later this week," M.J. said as she left his office.

She went to the locker room where she changed into her running clothes, buckled on her gun belt and put on the stocking cap her mother had knit. She stuffed the matching scarf in her pocket and pulled on the Thinsulate gloves. Her father was right—they didn't interfere with her gun hand at all.

When she arrived at Doc's camp, Lola was beside herself. She kept turning around, barking and wagging her tail uncontrollably. M.J. walked over and knelt down in front of her. "Look what I brought for you, girl," she said, removing the scarf from her pocket. She put it around Lola's neck and knotted it loosely to keep it from falling off. Lola sat down with an approving dog smile on her face, tail wagging harder than before.

Doc came out from inside the tent wearing the sweater M.J. had given him for Christmas. "Well aren't you two the coordinated fashion plates," he said.

"My mom made it for me for Christmas, but I'm not really a scarf person. I thought it would look good on Lola, though. What do you think?" she asked.

"I think you'd better not let your mother know that you gave your scarf to a dog," Doc said with a smile.

"Lola and I won't tell if you won't," she replied with a laugh. "How was your Christmas?"

"We had a very relaxing time," Doc said. "Went to the Christmas Eve party with the rangers and enjoyed a day to ourselves with no visitors in the park. I hope you had a nice time with your folks."

"I did, but I'm glad to be back. Missed seeing you guys and running with Lola," M.J. replied.

"We missed you too, M.J. Now take Lola for a run so she can show off her new scarf. I'll see you when you get back," Doc said.

They ran down the Old Carriage Road and over the Ridge Trail to Difficult Run. As her father would say, the wind and temperature made it "brisk," but after a couple of miles M.J. warmed up and so did Lola. The only people on the trails were hardy locals who were bundled up against the cold. Several people stared at Lola with her scarf and smiled.

The winter continued to be cold and there were several snow storms. She called her parents on New Year's Day and Ronceverte had already had a total of four and a half feet of snow, which was more than its yearly average.

She stopped by Dodd's office a few weeks later and he reported that the mountains to the west and north were already loaded with snow. "This could be bad," he said. "All depends on the temperatures in April."

M.J. and Lola continued to run, sometimes slogging their way through ankle-deep snow. By early March, the snow had melted and the temperatures were beginning to rise. The beginning of April set near-record high temperatures throughout the region and when she stopped in Dodd's office he said, "We should start to see the Potomac rising in about a week when all the streams upriver start filling up with melted snow water. Now it's just a question of how much."

"Do you think it will flood the whole park?" she asked.

"Probably at some point," he replied. "Mather Gorge will probably fill up before that, though. I plan to keep an eye on data from the gauging stations near the Appalachian foothills.   That should give us some warning of what to expect."

"Well, on a personal note," M.J. said, "this will probably complicate my life a little.   May be hard to run on all the trails, but the bigger problem may be getting to my office.   It sits in the park right along the Anacostia River and we may be treading water there too."

CHAPTER NINETEEN

The Anacostia River had risen enough to flood the park along its banks, but had not yet reached the parking lot at Anacostia Station. M.J. left her apartment early with the idea of checking in at the office before any real flooding occurred.

She was headed up the GW when Dispatch called on the radio. There had been another murder in Great Falls Park. Jake and Zerk had been notified and Eagle One would be airborne in about twenty minutes. M.J. turned on her flashing lights and siren and accelerated, dodging the early morning commuter traffic.

Her cell phone rang.

"M.J., this is Dodd," he said, pausing. "It was Doc."

She gasped, fighting back tears and trying to focus on her driving. "The dog?" she asked.

"I'm afraid she was killed too," Dodd replied. "It happened on Difficult Run, not far from where the boys were killed."

M.J. couldn't speak for a moment. She fought to compose herself, and then said, "I'll be there in about fifteen minutes."

She went even faster, concentrating on her driving to distract from the wave of emotion that threatened to paralyze her every thought and action. *C'mon M.J.*, she told herself, *Get yourself under control. Be a detective. Do this for Doc and Lola.*

She entered Georgetown Pike, passing several cars on double yellow lines with barely enough room to avoid hitting oncoming traffic. She was gripping the steering wheel so tightly that her fingers were becoming numb. "OK, M.J.," she said out loud, "Cool it or you're going to kill someone." She slowed to a speed that allowed her to negotiate the sharp turns without sliding into the bumper-to-bumper commuter traffic in the oncoming lane.

When she reached the parking lot for Difficult Run, she skidded to a stop, opened the door, leapt out and started running toward the trail. She passed several uniformed Fairfax County officers and went by them without stopping or speaking.

Down the trail there were two Park Police officers standing with Dodd. They had stretched crime scene tape between two trees. M.J. ran past them and quickly slipped under the tape. She could see Doc's body about fifty feet ahead near the stream side of the trail.

She suddenly remembered that in her rush she had forgotten to grab latex gloves from her car. Zerk would have some, but she wasn't going to wait. She started walking towards Doc's body, being careful to avoid anything on the trail that might be evidence.

When she got closer, she saw Lola lying limp and motionless with her back against a rock outcropping on the other side of the trail. Her teeth were bared in a frozen snarl and there was what appeared to be blood on them.

She turned her attention to Doc's body, which was chest down on the trail with his head turned to the side at an unnatural angle—not as far as the boys' had been, but close. Nearby was a flashlight, a towel and a plastic basket with its contents strewn on the trail.

Jake and Zerk arrived and she walked back toward the crime scene tape. Seeing Doc's and Lola's bodies had actually dampened her initial emotional response and helped her replace it with the dispassionate mindset of a criminal investigator.

Jake walked up to her, took her aside and said, "You look like you've been crying."

"I have been," she said. "The victims are the homeless guy I told you about and the dog I ran with in the park."

"Are you going to be OK to deal with this?" he asked.

"I *have* to be OK to deal with this," she answered, "but you back me up and let me know if I'm screwing anything up."

M.J. turned to Zerk, who handed her some gloves. "It looks like the dog—her name is Lola—got a bite of whoever did this, so be sure and get some swabs of her teeth," she said.

Zerk nodded and went under the tape, carrying his field kit. M.J. walked over to Dodd and asked, "What do you think happened?"

"An early morning hiker found them and called 911," Dodd said. "From the looks of it, Doc brought Lola down here to give her a bath in one of the pools in the stream. May have wanted to take a bath himself at the same time. I know he did that from time to time. Always came over at night when nobody was around."

"That makes sense. I saw the bottle of shampoo he used for Lola lying on the trail," M.J. said. "After we finish up here, I need to go up to his camp and look around.   I'd appreciate it if you'd come with me."

"Sure, M.J.," he replied. "I'll be in my office."

"Thanks," she said, pulling on the gloves while ducking under the tape.

Zerk had already taken several pictures and was kneeling down by Lola. He took a sterile swab from his kit and ran it over the dog's teeth. "Sure does look like blood," he said, examining the swab before placing it in an evidence bottle. "Maybe we'll luck out and get a DNA match."

"I sure hope so," M.J. said, kneeling down next to Zerk. She reached out and gently patted Lola's side with her gloved hand. "Good work girl," she said.

Jake was standing by Doc's body, examining the items scattered on the trail. His attention was drawn to the flashlight and he used his hand to shield the lens from the sunlight while he bent over it. "The flashlight was on when he was murdered, unless the killer turned it on afterward. The bulb is still glowing," he said.

M.J. came over and looked at the flashlight. "I doubt that the killer would turn it on and leave it on," she said. "More likely that Doc was using it to find his way up the trail."

She looked at the other items on the ground. In addition to the dog shampoo there was a bar of soap, a brush and the leash that they used when she and Lola ran together. Doc was fully clothed and his hair appeared damp. His eyes were partially closed and his face bore an almost serene expression.

Zerk came over and said, "No footprints, of course—same hard-packed gravel surface—and I don't see any blood there either. I'll get pictures of everything but I don't see much in the way of evidence except for the blood on the dog's teeth."

M.J. and Jake moved out of the way so Zerk could take his pictures. The Fairfax County Police came on her radio to let her know that they had already started patrolling the park perimeter. The GW Station came on to tell her that two Park Police cruisers had stationed themselves at each end of the parking lot areas in the main park and two horse-mounted officers had started moving cross country through the surrounding forest.

Eagle One came on the radio. It was flying up the river over Mather Gorge and the pilot said, "We'll start looking around to the southwest. Doesn't look like anybody would even think of trying to go east across the river or down it. It's almost to the top of the gorge."

M.J. thanked the pilot and turned to Jake. "Same drill as before," she said, "and I don't think they'll find anybody this time either."

When Zerk had finished, he joined M.J. and Jake and they started walking back toward the parking lot. When they came to the two uniformed officers who were providing crime scene security, M.J. stopped and said, "When the M.E. van comes, I want the dog's body to go to the morgue with the man's, understood?" They both nodded.

At the parking lot, M.J. turned to Jake and Zerk and said, "Gentlemen, it appears that we are now dealing with a serial killer."

CHAPTER TWENTY

M.J. left Jake to manage the crime scene and coordinate with the Fairfax County Police. She drove to the Visitor Center and found Dodd sitting at his desk.

"This is just awful," he said. "You've got to find out who did this."

"I will, Dodd," she said, "and I may need your help doing it. We can talk about that later. Right now, I need you to come with me to Doc's camp. I don't think we'll find anything, but I have to look around anyway and I need a witness."

They left the Visitor Center and cut over to the Old Carriage Road. When they reached the path off the Swamp Trail to Doc's camp, M.J. almost expected to see Lola at the top of the hill, wagging her tail like she always did. Of course, that wasn't going to happen now or ever again and that made M.J. profoundly sad, but she forced her feelings into the background for the moment.

Before they started up the path, M.J. stopped and looked to see if there were any unfamiliar footprints. Seeing none, she led the way up to the clearing.

She reached into her pocket and took out two pairs of latex gloves. She pulled on one pair and handed the other pair to Dodd and said, "Here, you'll need to put these on."

She surveyed the scene outside the tent, looking for anything unusual. There was nothing out of place. The two chairs were under the tent awning with the little table where Doc placed his book and coffee cup in between. There were two bowls outside the tent door for Lola's food and water, and the makeshift shelf had the usual items on it, except for those she had seen at the scene of the murder. The stove where Doc made coffee and heated food was just outside the awning.

They went inside the tent. She had never been in there before, but it was much as she had imagined it. There was a folding cot where Doc slept and a blanket folded and laid on the tent floor next to the cot for Lola. Hanging over the cot was a battery powered lantern, which appeared to be the only source of interior illumination. There was a small kerosene space heater and a bookcase fashioned from unfinished boards. On its top shelf was a picture of an elderly couple, who M.J. assumed were Doc's parents.

The other shelves contained books from the library in Great Falls Village, Alcoholics Anonymous *Twelve Steps and Twelve Traditions*, some writing paper, and a tin can full of pencils. There were makeshift hooks along the sidewall of the tent. Some of Doc's clothes were hanging there and on one hook was the scarf that M.J. had presented to Lola. She found the rest of Doc's clothes in a large rucksack propped against the foot of the cot. There were two cardboard storage boxes full of papers in the corner.

"Let's take these back to your office," she said, pointing to the boxes. "I think I've seen everything I need to see here."

"I'll have the rangers come up later and break down the camp," Dodd said. "I guess we can give a lot of this stuff to charity."

"I think Doc would have liked that," M.J. said, removing Lola's scarf from its hook and placing it in her pocket.

They each carried one of the boxes back to the Visitor Center. There was a small conference room adjacent to Dodd's office. "We can just work in here," he said.

"You go through your box and I'll go through this one," she said. "Keep your gloves on, please."

M.J. opened the box and took out several bundles of letters from Doc's parents. She didn't read them, feeling that they were too personal and had no possible bearing on the investigation. There were also several stacks of pictures. Some were of Doc and his parents; in none of them were there any other children. There were also some pictures of Doc in the Navy, including several that appeared to have been taken in Vietnam. It was the same Doc she knew, but forty-plus years younger. He was, she thought, a handsome and obviously serious young man.

M.J. looked up. Dodd was reading something in a blue, leather-bound folder. On the table in front of him was an open box about the size of a wallet, covered in the same blue leather material.

"M.J.," he said, "look at this."

She got up and walked to the end of the conference table where Dodd was sitting. The box contained a medal with an attached dark blue ribbon that had a white stripe down the middle.

"What is it?" she asked.

"This is the Navy Cross. It's the second highest decoration that can be awarded for valor. Here, read this," he said, handing her the blue folder.

She read the words:

> *The President of the United States takes pleasure in presenting the Navy Cross to Thomas Wonders, Hospital Corpsman Second Class, United States Navy, for extraordinary heroism while serving with the Second Battalion, Fifth Marines, First Marine Division, Fleet Marine Force, Quang Tin Province, Republic of Vietnam on June 2, 1967. . .*

It went on to relate how Doc had crawled onto a battlefield to treat several wounded Marines, helped drag two of them back to safety and had been wounded several times himself in the process. He had then gone back to treat more wounded and exposed himself to even more enemy fire.

The citation ended with: *By his outstanding courage and exceptional fortitude, Corpsman Wonders served to inspire all who observed him and upheld the highest traditions of the United States Naval Service.*

"He never said anything about this," M.J. said.

"I don't think Doc was the type to tell war stories or brag about his experiences," Dodd said. "I'll tell you this much, though: Whoever killed him murdered a real hero."

"That's just one more reason to catch the son of a bitch," M.J. said. "Let's finish going through these boxes."

When they had finished, M.J. turned to Dodd and said, "If it's OK, I'd like to keep these here for the time being. Now, let's talk about finding out who did this. I think we're dealing with somebody who may have killed at least once before the boys' murders. I've already checked Fairfax County records and the National Crimes Database for similar murders, but haven't found anything. I have a hunch that there may have been previous murders that looked like accidents or unexplained disappearances, meaning they were never reported as homicides. You have log books that would show incidents in the park, right?" she asked.

"Sure," he said. "They go all the way back to 1966 when it first became part of the national park system. Before that, it was owned by Fairfax County and before that it was privately owned. Of course, we have a lot of accidents every year. Like I told you, there are anywhere from eight to a dozen drownings on average, then there are people falling off the rocks and things like that."

"I'm looking for deaths or disappearances under questionable circumstances," M.J. said. "For now, I'd like to concentrate on any that may have occurred on Difficult Run in the five years before the boys were murdered. If you can start searching the logs, I'm going to check with Fairfax County about any reports they may have received."

"That would be a good idea," Dodd replied. "A lot of times the county gets the call and does the investigation and we never hear about it."

M.J. helped Dodd bring stacks of log books from the shelves in his office to the conference room table. She paged through one of them and saw multiple entries for each day which covered everything from the number of visitors to the water level in the river. Occasionally, there would be an entry noting some sort of accident, everything from twisted ankles to burns from a grill in the picnic area. She estimated that there were several hundred such entries in any given year.

"I appreciate you doing this," she said. "I'm going to go start on the Fairfax County records, but I'll be back later this afternoon."

"Glad to help in any way I can, M.J. I'll be here when you get back," Dodd said.

As M.J. was walking to her car, Jake called on the radio. Eagle One had left after about an hour without finding anything. Same for the Fairfax County patrols along the perimeter roads and the two horse-mounted Park Police officers. The van from the M.E. had arrived a short time ago and was loading the bodies of Doc and Lola.

She took out her cell phone and called Ted Sommers at Fairfax County Police. "Hello, Ted. This is M.J. from the Park Police. I need another favor. I'm looking for any suspicious incidents at Great Falls Park going back several years. Strange accidents, missing persons, that sort of thing," she said.

"Best place to go is our Central Records Division. Head of it is Becky Whitmer. I'll call and let her know you'll be stopping by. It's right across from the parking garage," he said. "I'm guessing this has something to do with the most recent murder in the park. Heard about it this morning on our radio traffic."

"Your guess is right. This appears to have been the same killer and I'm thinking there may have been an earlier homicide that didn't look like a homicide," she replied.

"Sounds like a good theory, but you may be hard pressed to find enough detail in any reports to give you anything to go on," he said.

"I know, but even some kind of pattern would be helpful," she said.

"Gotcha. Let me know if you need anything else," Ted said.

Becky Whitmer was standing behind a counter when M.J. entered the building that housed the Central Records Division. She was around forty with dark hair that she wore up in a bun. She didn't wear much makeup and her wire-rimmed glasses gave her the look of a librarian. Fitting, M.J. thought, since she kept track of volumes of police records.

"You must be Detective Powers," she said.

"Please call me M.J.," M.J. said, holding out her hand.

"Good to meet you M.J. I'm Becky," she said, shaking M.J.'s hand. "Ted Sommers called and said you'd be stopping by. What are you looking for?" she asked.

"Well, missing persons, unexplained accidents, things like that in Great Falls Park," M.J. replied.

"We can probably help with the missing persons. Those reports get filed with us. Accidents—except car accidents, of course—don't always get reported to us unless there is some suspicion of criminal activity. They most likely are reported to Fire and Rescue and they keep their own records," Becky explained. "They put in an updated database system a little over a year ago and we can access it from here."

"Great," M.J. said. "Let's start with your system."

Becky sat down at a computer, pressed a few keys and a data entry screen came up. "How far back do you want to go?" she asked.

"Let's start with April 2000 and see what we find," M.J. replied.

Becky entered the information for the date range. There was a pull-down menu with different types of incident reports. She highlighted "Missing Person."

"Now the database doesn't list the park separately, so I'm just going to select Great Falls as the location," Becky said and pressed "Enter." Four reference lines appeared on the screen.

"Now you can highlight each of these and pull up an image of the report that was filed," Becky said. "If you want to print the report, just click on that box and it will come out on the printer over there in the corner. When you're finished with our system, just let me know and I'll tie you into the Fire and Rescue database."

M.J. highlighted the first entry and brought up the report. It was for a missing teenager from Great Falls who had been found the next day. The next entry was for a man who had disappeared in Great Falls Park in late April 2001. She pulled up the report.

The man, James "Jimmy" Ferguson of Vienna, Virginia, had had an argument with his wife and left in their car, which was found the next morning in the parking lot for Difficult Run. Fairfax County officers had searched the trail in the park and found an empty bottle of Jim Beam whiskey and a flashlight, but no Jimmy. The case was marked as open. She printed a copy of the report.

The next entry was for the elderly parent of a Great Falls resident who suffered from Alzheimer's and had wandered off during the night, but was found within a few hours.

The last entry was for another incident at Difficult Run in early May 2003. A young couple, Kenneth Young and Melissa Hampton, both in their twenties, had gone to Difficult Run at night for a romantic tryst. Melissa had become angered and left to go back to her car in the parking lot, where she fell asleep, apparently suffering from the effects of alcohol. When she awoke in the morning, her boyfriend had not returned and she walked back down the trail to find him. The blanket they had been lying on was still there, as were two empty wine bottles and the flashlight they had used the night before. Her boyfriend, however, was nowhere in sight. She returned to the parking lot and called 911.

There was a supplemental report dated in late May which reported that a body, identified as that of Kenneth Young, had been found floating in the Potomac south of Washington. It was presumed that he had fallen into Difficult Run stream and been swept away. M.J. printed the reports.

M.J. found Becky and had her bring up the Fire and Rescue database, which was similar to that of the police, but had a separate location for Great Falls Park. She entered the same date range and highlighted "Accident" in the pull-down menu. Close to a hundred entries appeared.

M.J. sighed. "This may take a while," she said.

The majority of the entries were for river rescues by the Volunteer Fire and Rescue unit from Great Falls Village, which had two powerful boats for that purpose. There were also several entries for medical emergencies in the park.

About halfway down the list, she found an entry for an accidental death on Difficult Run. A local amateur ornithologist—a "birder", as they're called—named Dewey McGarrity had gone there at night in early April 2004 to look for an owl species that he believed inhabited that part of the forest. An early morning hiker had found his body between some rocks below the trail. His camera, infrared flash and flashlight were lying on the trail. The EMS personnel from Great Falls Fire and Rescue responded to the hiker's 911 call and determined at the scene that McGarrity's neck was broken, presumably from the fall.   There was no further investigation of the incident. M.J. printed the report.

She didn't find any more entries from the database that were of interest. She thanked Becky and headed back to Great Falls Park.

Dodd was in the conference room paging through the logs. "Find anything?" he asked.

"Three incidents of interest," she replied, and gave him a summary of each. "How about you?" she asked.

"I found an entry for the birder in our log, but we got the information from Fire and Rescue, so yours is probably much more detailed. There is one other that may fit what you're looking for," Dodd said. He opened one of the log books that had a yellow marker sticking out.

"This is for the morning of April 8, 2000," he began. "A Hispanic woman showed up at the entrance gate nearly hysterical and unable to speak any English. One of the rangers is bilingual and interpreted for us. It seems that she had dropped her husband off in the parking lot for Difficult Run around sundown the day before. He was going to fish in the stream and the river, and she was supposed to pick him up around ten that night. She went back and he hadn't shown up, so she waited there until around midnight. When he still didn't show up, she went home—she had left their two young children with her sister—and came back in the morning to look for him. He wasn't in the lot, so she walked down the trail and found his fishing rod, lunch bucket and flashlight, but no sign of her husband. That's when she came to the gate."

"I didn't see any missing person report for that in the Fairfax County records," M.J. said.

"Well, it says here that we told her to call the police, but my guess is she never did. If she's an undocumented alien, she would have been afraid to involve the police in anything for fear of being reported to the immigration authorities," Dodd said.

"It makes me wonder how many other incidents there may be that were never reported. Not just undocumented aliens, but people without any family to file a report," M.J. said. "In any event, the ones we've found seem to establish a pattern."

"What's that?" Dodd asked.

"They all occurred in the spring, they all occurred at night and they all occurred on Difficult Run—just like the boys and Doc," M.J. replied.

M.J. drove back to Anacostia Station and did a preliminary report on Doc's murder. She went online and searched the archives of the two weekly papers that served Great Falls, *The Sun Gazette* and *The Connection*. Although she found several stories involving Great Falls Park, none of them involved suspicious accidents or disappearances. She also searched the Metro section of the *Washington Post*, but the only story she found was the one from the year before about the boys' murders.

It was late and she was exhausted. She went to her apartment, put a frozen dinner in the microwave and opened a beer. She took one sip and all of her repressed emotions from the deaths of Doc and Lola came bursting forth. She began to sob uncontrollably and didn't fight it at all.

CHAPTER TWENTY-ONE

M.J. got up early the next morning and drove to Great Falls Park. She changed into her running clothes and set out on a different route, one that did not take her near Doc's camp. Her emotional release of the night before had been cathartic, but she was aware that she also needed to establish a new routine for her runs without Lola.

She ran as fast as she could, not slowing for uphill climbs on the trails and staying focused on her stride and her breathing. By the time she returned to the Visitor Center, she had done close to six miles. She was breathing heavily and sweating profusely, but she also felt cleansed. Running had always had that effect on her. She remembered doing the same kind of intense run when she learned of her grandmother's death. In a sense, it had provided the punctuation to that unhappy episode in her life, much as today's run had for the loss of Doc and Lola.

She showered, changed into her work clothes and stopped by Dodd's office.

"I didn't find anything else in the logs," he said, standing up from his desk.

"By the way," he said, "I started the paperwork to have Doc buried at Arlington National Cemetery. I talked to the folks at the mortuary—I know them from when they handled the arrangements for my wife—and they said they'd be willing to fix Lola up too and put her in the casket with Doc. They're not supposed to do that but . . . " His voice cracked and she could see tears forming in his eyes. " . . . she's a hero too, trying to protect Doc and all, don't you think?" Dodd asked.

"Yes, I do, and I know Doc would want it that way and so would Lola," M.J. replied, feeling tears forming in her own eyes. She walked over to Dodd and hugged him.

They both sat down and remained silent for several minutes. M.J. was the first to speak.

"Thanks for doing that, Dodd," she said, "and thanks for helping me with the investigation."

"Have you found out anything else?" he asked.

"I should get some forensics back this afternoon and I'll let you know what we find out. I went through the archived articles in the local papers last night and didn't find anything, but I have the feeling there may be more unreported incidents out there. Is there anyone local that might know something?" M.J. asked.

Dodd thought for a moment and said, "There's an older woman who lives in the village. Her name is Olive Coppin and she's lived here all of her life. I've met her several times at community meetings. She's in her late eighties, but still very sharp and knows just about everything that's ever happened in Great Falls. If you want, I can give her a call and set up a meeting for you."

"I'd appreciate that. Any time tomorrow would be fine," M.J. said.

"Will do, Dodd replied. "I'll let you know the time when I talk to you tomorrow."

M.J. drove to Anacostia Station. The message light on her desk phone was blinking. There were two messages: one from Zerk, the other from Dr. Martin, the Medical Examiner. She called Zerk first.

"Hi Zerk. What do you have for me?" M.J. asked.

"Got the results back from the DNA lab on the blood on the dog's teeth," he said. "No matches in the database. Oh, and the technician said that the blood sample looked like it might have been corrupted somehow, maybe from the dog's saliva."

"Damn!" M.J. said. "Anything else?"

"Not much," Zerk said. "Took a lot of pictures. I'll send you a set for your file. Got some fingerprints off the bottles lying on the trail, but they're all the same and I'd bet they match those of the victim. No footprints; same as last time."

"Thanks, Zerk. Let me know if you come up with anything else," she said.

She called Dr. Martin.

"Hello Doctor, this is Detective Powers. What did you find?" she asked.

"Well, we did the autopsy this morning. The victim died from the same kind of trauma that killed the boys last year," he said, "the 'hangman's fracture', if you recall. Also the killer was most likely right-handed, same as before. There were some marks and abrasions where the killer grabbed the victim's head, but nothing very useful."

"What about the dog? Was her neck broken too?" M.J. asked.

"No, she died differently. I had a veterinarian come in and take a look. It appears that she was picked up and thrown into the rock wall with such force that it broke her spine," he said.

"Would that be a quick death?" M.J. asked for her own sake.

"Definitely. She wouldn't have known what hit her. We saw some blood stains on her teeth and the report says you took a DNA sample. Any luck?" Dr. Martin asked.

"Unfortunately, no. The lab said there was no match and that the sample may have been contaminated with the dog's saliva," M.J. replied.

"Well, that's certainly possible," Dr. Martin said. "Anyway, I'm going to release the bodies today."

"The mortuary will be picking them both up," M.J. said. "Oh, and Doctor, I have another question not related to these murders but to the case in general."

"Sure. What is it?" he asked.

"I've got two deaths that were called accidental at the time, but I think they may have actually been homicides. Would your office have performed autopsies in such cases?" she asked.

"We generally don't do autopsies unless the cause of death is suspicious," Dr. Martin replied. "If these were treated as accidental, it's very doubtful that an autopsy was requested. If the bodies were buried, you could always try to get an exhumation order. If you're looking for neck trauma like the other cases, we could probably still make some type of determination if the bodies are in good enough shape."

"I'd have to check on that, but one of the bodies was in the Potomac for two weeks," M.J. said.

"Probably better take that one off the exhumation list," Dr. Martin said. "After being in the water that long, we're lucky to even be able to identify a body as being human remains.   Between the catfish and the snapping turtles, there's just not much left to examine."

"I see," said M.J. "Thanks again for your help."

Next, she called Dodd and filled him in on the results of the autopsy and DNA test.

"Doesn't sound very encouraging, M.J.," he said.

"Well, it does pretty well confirm that we're dealing with the same killer, but I think we'd already figured that out," she said. "By the way, the M.E. has released the bodies, so you might want to let the mortuary know."

"I'll do that. Also, I got in touch with Olive Coppin. She can see you tomorrow morning around nine. Stop by here in the morning and I'll give you directions to her house," Dodd said, adding, "She wanted to know what it was about and I just told her you were investigating some things and I thought she might be able to help."

"I'll see you in the morning," M.J. said.

CHAPTER TWENTY-TWO

The next morning, M.J. went to the park early and took a long run. She showered and changed into her regular clothes, then stopped by Dodd's office.

"Good morning, M.J.," he said. "Mrs. Coppin lives at 700 Ellsworth Avenue. It's in the old part of Great Falls. Second street on the right after you pass through the stoplight in the village."

On the corner of Dodd's desk was a pile of clothes, a pair of hiking shoes and the case containing the Navy Cross medal. He pointed to them and said, "I got those out of Doc's things to take to the mortuary. Do you think they're OK?" he asked.

"They're just fine. That's the way he dressed every day," M.J. replied. "Just a minute, I need to get something."

She went to her car, reached into the back seat and took out Lola's blue scarf, which she had left there two days before. She went back into Dodd's office and placed the scarf on top of the pile of Doc's clothing.

"Would you ask them to put this around Lola's neck and just knot it loosely," she said.

"I sure will, M.J. I'm probably going to take the stuff over there later this morning when I take them the paperwork for the casket and burial," Dodd said.

"I'll let you know how things go with Mrs. Coppin," M.J. said.

When M.J. arrived at the house, a 1950s-style brick ranch, Olive Coppin was plucking weeds from the front garden. She was wearing a cotton sun dress and sturdy sandals.

She took off her work gloves, walked over to M.J.'s car and shook her hand. "Hi, I'm Ollie," she said. "Dodd said you'd be coming by. My, you're a pretty young thing."

"Well, thank you Mrs. Coppin," M.J. replied.

"Oh, please call me Ollie," she said. "Let's go out on the back porch and talk there. I made some coffee if you'd like some, or I can make tea if you'd like."

"Coffee's fine, Ollie," M.J. said.

Ollie Coppin didn't look her age. Maybe mid-seventies, but certainly not late eighties. She was around five feet six inches tall and very trim. Her hair was silver and M.J. suspected from the cut that she took some pride in her appearance. Her voice was pleasantly high-pitched, almost lilting, and she smiled when she spoke. She reminded M.J. of her grandmother.

They walked through the living room to the kitchen, where Ollie poured a cup of coffee for each of them. The screened-in porch ran the full width of the back of the house and was shaded by two large oak trees. It was furnished with wicker furniture and there were planters containing ferns in each corner.

"So, how can I be of help?" Ollie asked.

"Well, I'm investigating some murders that occurred last year and just recently on Difficult Run. We believe they may be the work of the same person and Dodd has been helping me look for any suspicious accidents or disappearances that may have occurred in the past. We think it's possible this person may have committed other murders that went undetected. We thought you might know about some incidents that we may have missed," M.J. said.

"Well, I read about those boys that were found last year and someone said that a homeless man had been found on Monday. Are those the ones you're investigating?" Ollie asked.

"Yes, they are," M.J. replied. "One of the suspicious incidents we've found so far involved a man from here in Great Falls named Dewey McGarrity. Did you know him?" she asked.

"Sure. All of us old-timers knew Dewey. He was our resident naturalist," Ollie replied. "For what it's worth, by the way, I never did buy that business about him falling and breaking his neck. Dewey was about as sure-footed a person as I ever met and he was down in Great Falls Park almost every day, a lot of times on Difficult Run. He probably knew that trail as well as the walk up to his house."

"Is he buried here in Great Falls?" M.J. asked.

"Oh, Heavens no!" Ollie replied. "Dewey would never want to pollute the earth with his embalmed remains. As he requested in his will, he was cremated and his ashes were scattered just below the falls."

So much for exhuming that body, M.J. thought. "Can you think of any other suspicious incidents on Difficult Run?" she asked.

"Well, for whatever reason, there have always been strange happenings down there. How far back do you want to go?" Ollie asked.

"We looked at records going back to 2000, but we'd be interested in anything before that too," M.J. said.

"Let me see," Ollie said, "there was one in 1996, as I recall. A local handyman named Curt Wiley. He spent most of his evenings drinking with his buddies at the bar in the Old Brogue—that's our local pub. Well, when it came time to pay the bill he reached for his wallet and it was missing. He'd been hiking that afternoon on Difficult Run and figured it must have dropped out of his pocket. He told his friends to cover his tab, that he was going to go look for it and he'd pay them back. So he left—it was probably around nine or ten o'clock—and headed for Difficult Run. He didn't come back that night and the next morning they found his car in the Difficult Run parking lot. When his friends went looking for him, they found his wallet and a flashlight beside it on the trail, but no sign of him. They notified the police, but they figured he must have fallen in the stream and been swept away into the Potomac. I suppose the fact that he'd been drinking probably influenced their thinking on that score."

"Did they ever find his body?" M.J. asked.

"No, they didn't. But you probably know about the currents and how they sometimes pin bodies to the bottom and they never surface," Ollie replied.

"What time of year was this?" M.J. asked.

"It seems to me it was in the spring because they said the stream was pretty high and running very fast due to the rain," Ollie replied.

"Any others that you can recall?" M.J. asked.

"Well the only ones I would know about would involve people who lived in Great Falls, unless there was something in one of the newspapers," Ollie said. "The only other one that comes to mind right now occurred a long time ago, and when I say 'long' I mean well before you were born and maybe even before your parents were born."

"What year would that have been?" M.J. asked.

"1942," she replied.

M.J. smiled and said, "That's a little outside the time range we're looking at, but please tell me anyway."

"Well, that was back when the land was still privately owned and there was actually a road that ran along Difficult Run where the trail is now—big enough to drive a car on," Ollie began. "There was a little cabin down at the end— close to where the stream spills into the Potomac—that belonged to a family named Murphy that lived here in Great Falls—it was actually called Forestville in those days. The cabin had been in the family for years. Well, anyway, the whole family—they had two young daughters—was down at the cabin one night, just enjoying the beginning of spring weather I guess, when Mr. Murphy thought he heard something outside and went to investigate. He took a kerosene lantern and started walking down the road toward the river. Mrs. Murphy and the girls just stayed inside because it was raining pretty hard. Well, when Mr. Murphy had been gone for a good long while, his wife went out to look for him. She saw the lantern down the road and thought it was him, but when she called out, he didn't answer. She walked down a way and saw the lantern lying in the road but didn't see him anywhere. She became frightened and ran back to the cabin, grabbed the girls and took off in the car to find help."

Ollie continued, "She got ahold of the Fairfax County Police, but they had only been in existence for a couple of years and didn't have but two or three officers. By the time they arrived, it was near daybreak. When they went down the road they saw Mr. Murphy's footprints going from the cabin toward the river. Then they found the lantern and, because of all the mud, they were able to see some other footprints that seemed to come from the hill on the north side of the road. At that point, Mr. Murphy's footprints turned toward the stream. If I recall, they said it looked like he was running. In any event, there was no sign of Mr. Murphy."

"Did they ever find him?" M.J. asked.

"Well, they spotted his body pinned between some rocks about a quarter mile down the Potomac, but the water was so high and fast they couldn't get to it for a couple of days," Ollie replied.

"What did they think had happened?" M.J. asked, now thoroughly enthralled with the story.

"They thought he might have been attacked by a drifter that was living in the park," Ollie replied. "This was just a few years after the Great Depression and a lot of folks were still out of work and homeless. Funny thing, though, when they finally recovered the body, his wallet and money were still in his pants pocket. Didn't seem to me, even then, like someone was trying to rob him."

"Did they ever determine how he had died?" M.J. asked.

"I don't know if they did an autopsy or anything, but somebody told me his body had been thrashed around in the river so much that his head was turned all funny," Ollie replied.

This got M.J.'s attention, but she was having difficulty dealing with the possibility of a serial killer who would now be in his eighties or nineties. She made a mental note to look into it further, but for now decided to turn the conversation to less morbid topics.

"Have you lived in Great Falls all your life?" she asked.

"Oh yes," Ollie replied. "Of course, like I said, it was called Forestville back then. They didn't change the name to Great Falls until 1955. We lived in a house on Georgetown Pike near what is now Old Dominion Drive. When I was little, though, it's where the trolley tracks ran for the Great Falls and Old Dominion Railroad. There was a station house right there on the corner and another one down in Great Falls Park, which the railroad owned.

"My sister Sarah and I went to the old schoolhouse on down Georgetown Pike toward the village—it's still there as a 'historic structure.'" She laughed and said, "Guess that makes me 'historic' too."

M.J. smiled and asked, "What was the park like back then?"

"Oh, it was really something," Ollie said. "People would come from Washington and points south on the trolley cars all day long and into the evening—hundreds and hundreds of them. The women all wore beautiful long dresses and big hats, and the men were in suits and ties wearing bowlers and skimmer hats. The park had a big picnic ground, the Great Falls Inn, a carousel and a dance pavilion—why it even had a little zoo!"

"A zoo? What kind of animals?" M.J. asked.

"Well, let's see," Ollie replied, "there were some native animals that kids could actually pet—rabbits, goats, that sort of thing. Then there were a bunch of animals that had been brought in from Africa—a zebra, some ostriches, a wildebeest. Oh, yes, and an ape of some sort that they brought in sometime in early '36. I think they thought it would be a big attraction."

"An ape? Was it a gorilla?" M.J. asked.

"No, it wasn't a gorilla," Ollie replied. "I read every issue of *National Geographic* I could get my hands on and I never saw a picture of an ape like this one. This thing was as big as a gorilla, close to six feet tall when it stood up. But its face wasn't all smushed in like a gorilla. It looked more like the face of a chimpanzee; you know, lighter in color with pink lips and rounded features. I'll tell you something else, it was mean as all get out. Boys would shine lights in its eyes and it would grab the bars on its cage and bare its teeth, ready to kill them. Mr. Miller, who managed the park, had to put up a fence so people couldn't get too close."

"So you were here when the Great Flood of 1936 happened?" M.J. asked.

"Oh my, yes. I'll never forget it!" Ollie replied. "We were at our house and Mr. Miller went racing by in his Model-T headed for the park—I guess he'd gone home for supper. You could hear people yelling and screaming down in the park and the sound of cars farther down Georgetown Pike trying to all get out at once—the trolley had gone out of business a few years before, so by then most people came by automobile. Well, anyway, my sister and I just had to see what was going on, so we got on my bicycle—I was pedaling and she was on the handlebars—and we went zooming down the path that ran next to the trolley tracks. My parents would have killed us if they'd known we were doing it!

"Well, anyway, when we got down to the old trolley station, we jumped off the bike and ran out onto the little observation deck. What a sight! The water was already over the entire area and you could see that it was rising really fast. People were running to their cars and some were just running up to higher ground. The water reached the dance pavilion and its floor started to lift up. It didn't take long before it began to float away toward the river. If it hadn't been for two big trees, it would have gone right down the Potomac.

"Then we saw Mr. Miller running up from the Old Carriage Road—I guess he couldn't get his Model-T by all the cars trying to get out. He started running around the park yelling at people to leave, then he took off toward the zoo, which was up on a little knoll away from the rest of the park. The water was still rising really fast and it was going to reach the animals in a matter of minutes, so he ran along opening up the pens and shooing them out so they could get to safety. But when he got to the ape cage, he didn't try to shoo them out. He just took off the lock and ran away as fast as he could."

"Them?" M.J. asked. "There was more than one?"

"Yes," Ollie replied. "There was a big one and a smaller one. They said they were a male and a female."

CHAPTER TWENTY-THREE

M.J. stayed and listened to Ollie a little while longer. She and her sister had watched until the rising water threatened the trolley station where they were standing. All of the released animals had fled into the forest, including the apes, which had easily pushed open the door to their cage.

It took several days for the flood waters to recede and when they did most of the animals had begun wandering back toward the zoo. Several had to be tracked down and led back, but eventually they were all returned to their enclosures—all, that is, but the apes, who were nowhere to be found. Mr. Miller had searched for them in the deep forest for several days without luck, but he had died of a heart attack about two weeks after the flood and no one else ever took up the task of finding the apes.

As M.J. was leaving, she said, "Thank you for providing so much information. May I come back and visit if I have any more questions?"

"Any time, dear. I'm usually right here at the house, so just stop by," Ollie replied.

"One other thing," M.J. said. "What was Mr. Murphy's first name?"

"Kevin, I believe," Ollie replied.

"Thank you again," M.J. said.

M.J. headed back to Great Falls Park. As she drove, she processed her conversation with Ollie Coppin, trying to figure out how, or really *if*, it might fit into her investigation. She kept replaying in her head her father's quote from Sherlock Holmes: *When you have eliminated the impossible, whatever remains, however improbable, must be the truth.*

When she pulled into the parking lot at the Visitor Center, Dodd was walking to his car. He put the stack of clothes and a file folder on the passenger seat and walked over to M.J.

"How'd things go with Mrs. Coppin?" he asked.

"What a nice lady," M.J. replied. "I got a lot of good information and I'm going to follow up on a few things. Can I use the phone in your office while you're gone?" she asked.

"Sure," he replied.

"I'll stop by in the morning and tell you some more about the conversation," she said.

"See you then," Dodd said as he climbed into his car.

M.J. sat down at Dodd's desk. Her first call was to Becky Whitmer at Fairfax County Police Central Records Division.

"Hello Becky, this is M.J. Powers from the Park Police. I was in the other day," she said.

"Sure, M.J. What can I do for you?" Becky said.

"Well I have a favor to ask," M.J. said. I'm looking for a report on a suspected homicide in the spring of 1942."

"Wow! You're really going back! We have reports from then; they're just not in the computerized database. I can check the hard copy files for you though. What's the name and approximate date?" Becky asked.

"The victim was Kevin Murphy of Forestville. The incident probably occurred in April or May of '42," M.J. replied.

"I'll take a look and let you know," she said.

"Thanks. If you find anything, just e-mail it to the address on the card I gave you," M.J. said.

Next, M.J. called Dr. Martin at the Medical Examiner's office.

"Hello, Doctor. This is Detective Powers. I have a favor to ask," she said.

"Sure, Detective, what is it?" he asked.

"There may have been an autopsy performed in a suspected homicide case in 1942. I'd like to get a copy if possible," she said.

"Well, this office didn't even exist in 1942. Autopsies were handled back then by the county coroner. All of the original records are at the Fairfax County Courthouse, but we have microfiche copies here, so we might be able to find it for you. What was the name of the deceased and around what date would the autopsy have been performed?" he asked.

She gave him the information, thanked him and asked that a copy be e-mailed to her. "If you find anything, can I give you a call to discuss it?" she asked.

"Always glad to talk to you, Detective. You seem to be going pretty far back if this is the same investigation we discussed before," he replied.

"It's the same investigation and, yes, this is further back than I ever imagined," she said.

Next, she got the number from information for the National Zoo. When she identified herself and asked to speak with someone who dealt with apes, she was put through to Dr. Julia Matheson.

"Hello, Doctor Matheson. This is Detective Powers of the Park Police. I was wondering if I might stop by and ask you a few questions?" M.J. said.

There was a moment of silence, then Dr. Matheson replied somewhat curtly, "Does this have to do with some kind of investigation of the zoo or myself, because if it does I'll have to refer the matter to our legal counsel's office."

M.J. quickly replied, "Oh, no . . . nothing like that, Doctor. I just need some animal-related information for an investigation I'm conducting and I thought you might be a good person to talk to."

"Well, I can't imagine what help I could be, but if you want to stop by, I'll be in my office. It's right next to the Great Ape House," Dr. Matheson said.

M.J. arrived at the National Zoo about thirty minutes later, parked her car in the "Official Use Only" lot and walked to the Great Ape House, which was located toward the back of the sprawling complex. There was a small one-story brick building next to it with a sign that said "Offices – Not Open to the Public." M.J. entered the lobby and identified herself to the receptionist, who called Dr. Matheson on the intercom.

After a few minutes, a door opened and a petite, trim woman in her forties with dark, close-cropped hair entered. She extended her hand and said, "Detective Powers, I'm Dr. Matheson. Please, come back to my office."

The sign outside her office said "Julia Anne Matheson, D.V.M. – Chief Veterinarian." As they entered she said, "I'm sorry if I was a little snappy on the phone. We don't get many calls here from the police. Please, have a seat."

"That's quite alright, Doctor. I should have made myself more clear from the beginning," M.J. replied.

"So, what kind of information are you looking for?" Dr. Matheson asked.

"Actually," M.J. said, "I'm trying to identify a particular type of ape that's been described to me as large like a gorilla—almost six feet tall when it's erect—but has a facial structure and coloring more like a chimpanzee."

Dr. Matheson thought for a moment. "What you are describing sounds like a Bili Ape," she said.

"How is that spelled?" M.J. asked.

"It's spelled B-I-L-I, but pronounced *bee-lee*," Dr. Matheson replied.

"Do you have one here at the zoo?" M.J. asked.

"Definitely not, Detective," Dr. Matheson replied. "No one from the West has even seen one in at least forty years. May I ask why you need this information?"

"I can't really tell you that right now Doctor," M.J. replied. "It has to do with an ongoing investigation."

"Well, I guess I understand," Dr. Matheson said, "but I'm dying of curiosity and hope you'll get back to me when you can. Now, as for the Bili Ape, the person you should be talking to is Dr. Steve Peterson. He's a primatologist at the National Geographic Society and one of the leading authorities in the world on that species. If you like, I'll give him a call right now and see if he's available."

"I'd certainly appreciate that," M.J. said.

Matheson turned the knob on an old-fashioned Rolodex on her desk, flipped through some cards and then dialed a number on her phone.

"Hello, Steve. This is Julia Matheson at the National Zoo," she said. "I'm fine, thank you. I hope you're doing well too. Haven't seen you since we spoke at that conference in San Diego about a year ago. Listen, the reason for my call is I have a detective from the Park Police sitting in my office and she has some questions about Bili Apes . . . No, she couldn't tell me why and probably won't be able to tell you either, but I thought you would be the best person for her to talk to . . . That's great! I'll send her down. Hope to see you soon."

She turned to M.J. and said, "He's in his office and said he can see you now if that's convenient. He's in the main building on 17th Street."

"I know right where it is. Thank you for all your help," M.J. said and shook her hand.

M.J. drove directly to the National Geographic Society and parked about a block away. It was an imposing building with a red tile roof and columns over the main entrance. There was a long line of tourists waiting to enter, but M.J. bypassed them and used her badge to enter through the "Employees Only" door.

Dr. Peterson came down and met her in the lobby. He was easily six feet tall, thin, probably in his mid-forties, had curly salt-and-pepper hair and a neatly-trimmed beard. He wore wire-rimmed glasses that framed his deep-set brown eyes.

"Hi, Detective, I'm Steve Peterson," he said, extending his hand.

"Thanks for seeing me on such short notice," M.J. said as they shook hands.

"No problem. Let's go up to my office to talk," he said.

They used the elevator to reach his office on the third floor. The plaque on the door said "Stephen L. Peterson, Ph.D." It was a relatively small office, with a window that looked out on the busy 17th Street. His desk was piled with papers and the only wall treatment was a large map of the African continent.

"Please, have a seat," he said, pointing to the only chair that was not stacked with papers. "So, Julia says you want to know about Bili Apes and won't be able to tell me why."

"That's essentially correct," M.J. replied. "As I told Dr. Matheson, I'll be glad to explain the reason for my questions when I can, but right now that's not possible."

"Fair enough," he said. "So what, exactly, do you want to know?"

"Well, for starters, what exactly is a Bili Ape?" she asked.

"That's a good question," he replied, "and the answer is that we're not really sure. They are thought to be either a very large chimpanzee or a new species of gorilla with chimpanzee-like features. This has been the subject of a lot of discussion and research, but thus far there's no real consensus."

"Dr. Matheson said no one from the West has actually seen one, so I guess you haven't either," M.J. said.

"Unfortunately, that is correct," he replied. "I have been to the Democratic Republic of the Congo three times, specifically to search for the Bili Ape. I have yet to see one, although I have interviewed a lot of natives who claim they have. I have seen purported skulls, footprints, droppings and nesting areas, but no live animals. Part of the problem is even determining where they live. They used to inhabit the Bili Forest, from which they get their name, but all of the civil strife and deforestation in the region has probably driven them into the hills."

"Do you have a picture of one?" M.J. asked.

"Yes, I do. It is the only one that I consider authentic and was acquired in 1996 by a Swiss photographer and conservationist named Karl Ammann. It was taken by poachers using a motion-detecting trail camera. Give me just a second and I'll pull it up," he said, turning to his computer keyboard and typing in some information.

He turned the computer monitor toward M.J. It showed a very large dark-haired creature walking nearly upright on a jungle trail. Its face was light in color and its mouth was outlined by pink lips. Its hairline extended down its forehead to just above its eyes, making it look like a hood. She remembered Doc's description of the figure he had seen walking along the ridge in Great Falls Park during a rainstorm: . . . *he was pretty big . . . He was kind of hunched over, but I'd guess he was around six feet tall. Pretty hefty in the shoulders, but I couldn't see much detail. It looked like he was wearing a jacket or sweatshirt or something like that with a hood pulled up over up his head. ... I remember seeing his face sticking out from the hood and it looked white.*

"Could I have a copy of that picture?" M.J. asked.

"Sure," Dr. Peterson replied and pressed the print button on the keyboard. A color printer in the corner of the office sprang to life. He removed the page and handed it to M.J.

"Is it possible that any Bili Apes were brought to the United States in the early part of the 1900s?" she asked.

"During that time," he answered, "virtually every kind of African animal was being brought into this country. There was almost no regulation by the federal government and there was an active trade in what were referred to as 'exotic animals.' Some of the animals went to zoos but as many, and maybe even more, went to private owners. It is certainly not out of the question that what are now referred to as Bili Apes could have been captured and brought here. The Belgian

Congo, which is now the Democratic Republic of the Congo, was the prime location in Africa for big game hunters and animal trappers." He paused for a moment and then asked, "Do you have reason to believe that Bili Apes were brought here?"

"I really can't go into that, Dr. Peterson," M.J. responded.

"I can understand that, Detective, but if there is any possibility that a Bili Ape is being held in captivity in this country it would be of enormous importance to the field of primatology," he said.

"Doctor, I just can't provide any details on my investigation at this time. Trust me, as soon as I can, I'll let you know," M.J. said.

"I'll take you at your word on that," he said. "Any other information you need from me?"

She thought for a minute and then asked, "Just how strong are these apes?"

"Well, they must be quite powerful," he said. "The natives call them 'lion killers.'"

"They eat lions?" M.J. asked.

"Other way around," he replied. "Apes are prey for lions. Although apes are omnivorous, their meat diet is pretty much limited to rodents, birds, things of that size. No, I'd say that a Bili Ape would only kill a lion as a defensive maneuver."

M.J. could feel her heart pounding and she took an almost audible breath before asking her next question. "Just how do they kill the lions?" she asked.

"I've never seen it myself, of course," Dr. Peterson replied, "but I've interviewed several natives who claim they have. They all describe it the same way: The ape jumps onto the lion's back, grabs its head, pulls it back and then twists it violently to break its neck."

CHAPTER TWENTY-FOUR

M.J. sat in silence with her eyes wide. Dr. Peterson asked, "Everything alright, Detective?"

"Yes, yes . . . I'm just collecting my thoughts," she replied. "Do you have time for a few more questions?"

"Sure," he replied. "Fire away."

"How long do Bili Apes live?" she asked.

"We don't know exactly, because we haven't been able to study them. Generally, the great apes live about thirty-five to forty years in the wild. That would probably be a good estimate for the Bili," Dr. Peterson replied.

"How long before they reach maturity?" M.J. asked.

"Based on other apes, between seven and ten years for males; seven and eight years for females," he replied.

"How often do they give birth?" M.J. asked.

"Generally, the great apes produce a single offspring every four years," Dr. Peterson explained. "The gestation period is eight and a half months and the young can walk at three to six months."

"Do the offspring inherit traits from their parents, things like fear of humans?" M.J. asked.

"Well, they might inherit some traits, but a lot of traits are the result of the rearing process," Dr. Peterson replied. "Keep in mind that apes are very much like humans in most things, including the way they raise their young."

"Can they survive in a colder climate?" M.J. asked.

"I'm going to assume you're talking about a climate like we have here, which is considered moderate," Dr. Peterson replied, "and the answer is probably yes. Apes are very adaptable, as are most primates. They might grow more body hair for warmth and even start periods of hibernation during especially cold periods to conserve body heat and lower food requirements. They might also change their nesting habits. We believe the Bili is a ground nester, but that might change in a colder climate. Most likely, they would find a more confined space where they could huddle together for warmth. Some kind of cave or tunnel would probably make the most sense."

M.J. thought for a moment and asked, "Do apes inbreed?"

"Generally, no," Dr. Peterson responded. "The females instinctively know to seek mates from another group. Of course, if that's not possible because of restricted movement, they will inbreed. That's been observed in apes living in areas where their habitat has been reduced in size by the encroachment of humans."

"What are the effects of inbreeding?" M.J. asked.

"Once again, very much the same as in humans," Dr. Peterson replied. "At the very least, it would tend to amplify any bad traits that might have existed in the first place."

"What about aggressive behavior?" M.J. asked.

"Well, male apes are naturally aggressive," Dr. Peterson explained. "It has to do with territorial domination. Inbreeding could certainly make a male more aggressive. The females are not naturally aggressive, except when protecting their offspring, so it's hard to say what effect inbreeding would have on them."

"Can apes become psychopathic?" M.J. asked.

"Of course," he replied. "I can't stress strongly enough that the characteristics of apes will almost always be analogous to those found in humans and that would include psychopathic behavior. The larger non-human primates are so closely linked to humans that their DNA is about ninety-eight percent the same as ours."

That would explain the DNA results from the blood on Lola's teeth, M.J. thought. *It wasn't corrupted; it was just missing two percent of human DNA.*

"I think you've answered all of my questions for now, Doctor. If I think of anything else, can I give you a call?" M.J. asked.

"Sure, I'll give you my card," he replied, searching for one in the drawer of his desk. "Don't forget your promise to tell me what this is all about, Detective."

"I won't," M.J. said. "Thank you for taking the time to talk to me."

She drove to Ollie Coppin's house in Great Falls, unable to keep from replaying her conversation with Dr. Peterson during the trip. Ollie wasn't in the front yard, so M.J. went around the house to the back porch. She was sitting in a chair reading and looked up when she heard M.J.

"Well, how nice to see you again so soon," Ollie said.

"I'm sorry to bother you, Ollie, but I wanted to show you something," M.J. replied.

"No problem at all. Come on in," Ollie said.

M.J. opened the screen door and removed the picture from a manila folder. She handed it to Ollie and said, "Does this look like the ape that was kept at the park?"

Ollie took the picture and immediately said, "Why yes, that's it exactly. What is it?"

"It's called a Bili Ape and it probably came from what was then called the Belgian Congo," M.J. replied.

"Well I'll be," Ollie said. "Can you tell me why you're so interested in this ape?"

"Unfortunately I can't just yet Ollie," M.J. said, "but trust me, you have been a great help. Thank you again."

"Can you stay for coffee?" Ollie asked.

"I'd love to, but I have to get back to my office," M.J. replied. "I would certainly like to stop back another time, though."

"You are welcome here any time," Ollie said.

M.J. drove to Anacostia Station. It was about six o'clock and there were several other detectives working at their desks. M.J. checked her e-mail. There was one from Becky Whitmer. Attached to it was a scanned copy of the report on the suspected murder of Kevin Murphy in 1942. It had been written on a manual typewriter and had multiple cross-outs and smudges.

M.J. read the report quickly. It closely followed the narrative of the incident provided by Ollie Coppin, including the footprints found on the muddy road. It noted that from

Murphy's footprints he appeared to have been running away from his attacker and that the other set of footprints appeared to have been made by "a person of some size" based on their width. The final paragraph of the report said that Murphy's body had been recovered two days later and was taken to the county morgue.

There was also an e-mail from Dr. Martin with an attached copy of the autopsy report for Kevin Murphy. In the e-mail Martin said, "Please give me a call. I'll be working late tonight, probably at least until 9:00."

While she was opening the file with the autopsy report, M.J. dialed Martin's number.

"Hello, Detective," Dr. Martin said. "Glad you called. I read the autopsy report and looked at the pictures of the body and the x-rays that were with it. The autopsy was done by an assistant coroner, who appears to have been just a regular M.D. with no training in forensic pathology. Fortunately, he was very meticulous in recording his findings."

"Were you able to determine anything?" she asked.

"Yes, I think so," he said. "There were bruises to the neck which he concluded were caused by some form of blunt force trauma. You can actually see them in the pictures, which are a little faded but still usable. Fortunately, the body had only been in the water for a couple of days so the soft tissue wasn't too badly decomposed."

M.J. paged ahead to the pictures which showed Murphy's body on the autopsy table. There were bruises clearly visible on the sides of his neck. More striking to M.J. was the fact that his head was tilted backwards and appeared to be resting limply on its side.

Dr. Martin continued, "Now, the bruises by themselves might lead one to the conclusion that they were due to some sort of striking wound. But the doctor also found that there was a complete dislocation of the second and third cervical vertebrae. You can see this in the x-ray, which has deteriorated quite a bit but is still readable. He ascribed this to the fact that the body had been battered against rocks in the river for two days."

M.J. looked at the x-ray, which, to her, seemed very similar to those taken of the murdered boys' necks.

"To get to the point," Dr. Martin said, "I think his explanation for the dislocated vertebrae is totally wrong. No matter how much the body was thrown against rocks by a flooded river, it would not have resulted in that injury. Soft tissue trauma, yes; fractured vertebrae, maybe; completely dislocated cervical vertebrae, no. What you have here,

Detective, is a man who was murdered in exactly the same way as the more recent victims in your case. How that is possible after more than sixty years, I'll leave to your investigative skills. I just hope you'll let me know when you figure it out."

"You know, Doctor, a lot of people have been asking me to do that. I'll add your name to the list. Thanks for the help," she said.

M.J. drove to her apartment, stopping at a deli on the way to pick up a sandwich and two beers. When she went inside, she put the beers in the refrigerator, took a bite of the sandwich and then headed for the shower, where she stayed under the spray until her tense muscles relaxed. She put on a terrycloth robe, opened one of the beers and sat down at the counter in her kitchenette.

She slid a pad and pencil over from underneath the wall phone and began doing some rough calculations in her head while making notes on the paper: *If the male ape was ten years old and the female was, say, eight years old when they arrived at Great Falls Park in 1936, they could have produced offspring in as little as eight and half months. Not likely though,* she thought, *after the trauma of being shipped to the United States, being uprooted by the Great Flood and trying to adapt to their new surroundings in the park. Best case would probably be first offspring in '37 or '38, another in '41 or '42. The original apes probably died no later than the early '60s and their offspring no later than the '70s. That means that if there are apes still living in the park they would be the third generation and nearing the end of their life expectancy.*

She took a drink of beer and retrieved her sandwich from the end of the counter. She was exhausted and tomorrow was going to be another long day. She finished the sandwich and beer, turned off the lights and crawled under the covers on her bed.

Sometime during the night, she awakened from a nightmare in which she was being pursued by a giant ape. She rubbed her face and tried to go back to sleep.

CHAPTER TWENTY-FIVE

M.J. got up very early the next morning, which was not hard to do since she had never really gotten back to sleep after her nightmare. The sun was just coming up when she arrived at Great Falls Park. She changed clothes and set out for a long run.

When she had run before she had looked for suspicious people on the trails and in the park. Now she found herself focusing on the park's terrain. She noticed large clusters of rock in the forest, some with crevices big enough to shelter an ape, and dense foliage that obscured the underlying ground where a nest might be located.

Just where would these things live? she thought. *Wherever they lived, they would probably avoid coming out in the daytime because of all the people in the park. They and their ancestors had probably become strictly nocturnal animals, only venturing out when the park was closed and the people had left. That's when they would forage for food, returning to their nest before dawn.*

All of the murders had occurred at night and all in the spring or early summer, she thought. *But why had all of the murders taken place on Difficult Run? Did that mean that the apes had always lived in that part of the park or was it just happenstance? And, if they lived in that area, why were the murders confined to just that time of year? And what prompted the attacks in the first place? Dr. Peterson had said that the males were naturally aggressive. Were the attacks the result of some primordial need to assert territorial dominance? Or perhaps the attacker was not a male at all, but a female protecting her young.*

One thing was certain, she thought, *there remained many more questions than answers.* She knew she was going to need help in building a convincing case or no one would accept her solution to the murders.

After she had showered and changed into her work clothes, she went to Dodd's office. He was sitting at his desk going through a stack of papers.

"I need to talk to you," she said, "and it may take a while."

He pushed the stack of papers aside and said, "As much time as you need, M.J. Why don't you close the door."

"What I'm going to tell you I haven't shared with anyone else, not my partner or my boss . . . no one," M.J. said. "I'll need for you to keep it confidential until we figure out what to do, but most of all I need your help in making sense out of it."

"You know you can trust me, M.J. and I'll be glad to help in any way I can," he said.

She told him about her conversation with Ollie Coppin, her recollection of the escape of the two apes in 1936 and the suspected murder of Kevin Murphy in 1942. Then she told him about her meeting with Dr. Peterson at National Geographic and the conclusions of Dr. Martin about the cause of death in the Murphy case. She also showed him the picture of a Bili Ape.

As she spoke, Dodd's eyes grew wider and when she had finished he sat for several seconds staring at the picture without saying a word. Finally he said, "M.J., do you really think all these murders were committed by this creature or its ancestors?"

"I'm certain of it," she replied. "If you think about it, it's the only explanation given the span of time. It's also the only logical explanation of why the murders were committed the way they were."

Dodd thought for a minute, then said, "I think you're right, M.J. Now what can I do to help?"

"We need to do several things in short order," she said. "First, we need to go back as far as we can and look for any other suspicious deaths or disappearances on Difficult Run. I'll check the county records if you'll check the log books. Once we have that, we need to try to put everything together and figure out where these things live in the park. Then, we need to figure out how to prove they exist, because without that I'll never be able to sell this to my superiors."

"Well," Dodd said, "since this only became part of the national park system in 1966, I won't have any records before that. I stopped at the year 2000 last time, so I've got 34 more years to go through. That's going to take some time, but I'll get started right away."

"I'm going to check as far back as I can in the Fairfax County records," M.J. said. "We can cross-check what we come up with and maybe find some clues or a pattern."

M.J. drove to Fairfax County Police Central Records Division and found Becky Whitmer.

"I'm sorry to just show up like this Becky," M.J. said, "but some things have developed in that case I'm working on and I need to do another records search. How far back does your computer database go?" she asked.

"1960," Becky said. "The records before that—back to 1940 when the Department was formed—are all in hard copy, like the one I found for you yesterday. By the way, was that of any help?" she asked.

"More than you can imagine," M.J. replied. "It sounds like for records before 1960 I'd need a name or a date to find anything."

"Unfortunately, yes," Becky said. "One of these days—if we ever get the funding—we can put those old records in the system, too. Well, just sit down at the same computer you used last time and let me know if you have any questions."

"Do you know how far back the Fire and Rescue system goes?" M.J. asked.

"Well, I think the county department formed around 1949, but I'm guessing their system probably only goes back to 1960, like ours. The same company put both systems in, so that would make sense. I'll call my counterpart over there and see what I can find out," Becky replied.

M.J. sat down at the computer and entered the same search terms she had used before. For the period between January 1960 and March 2000 there were fourteen missing person reports for Great Falls, eight of which were related to the park. Five of those had been closed out because the person had been found; one contained a supplemental report; and the other two remained open.

M.J. looked at the first case, which involved the disappearance in mid-April 1972 of a photographer from Washington. He had gone to Difficult Run late at night to take time-lapse photos of the Potomac below Mather Gorge for a coffee table book he hoped to publish. When he didn't return by morning, his girlfriend contacted the police who found his car in the Difficult Run parking lot. When they checked the trail they found his camera and tripod knocked over next to his gear bag and a flashlight, but no sign of him. A supplemental report said that his body was found almost three weeks later floating in the tidal basin near the Jefferson Memorial. She printed a copy of the report.

The next case concerned the disappearance in late June 1985 of a confirmed alcoholic from Vienna, Virginia who left his home to go late-night drinking on Difficult Run. His credit card records showed that he had stopped at a state-run liquor store earlier in the evening and purchased a fifth of vodka. His car was found in the Difficult Run parking lot the next day, but police did not find a trace of him there or on the trail, not even the vodka bottle. His body was never recovered and it was assumed that he had fallen in the stream, been swept into the river and drowned. M.J. decided it was probably a case of someone rock hopping while under the influence, but she printed the report anyway.

The last case dealt with the disappearance of a resident of Falls Church, Virginia who went night fishing on Difficult Run in early May 1996. His fishing rod, tackle box and a flashlight were found on the trail, not far from where Doc was murdered. The body never surfaced and, due to the high water in the river, it was presumed to have been pinned to the bottom by the strong current. M.J. printed a copy of the report.

Becky returned and said, "I talked to the head of records for the Fire and Rescue Department. It's like I thought. Their computerized records only cover the same period as ours. She also said that their hard copy files before 1960 are kind of hit or miss because the volunteer departments kept their own records and didn't always turn in copies to headquarters. Here, I'll pull up their database and you can take a look."

M.J. entered the same dates. The database produced a list of several hundred reports for Great Falls Park. As before, many of them dealt with medical emergencies and there were multiple rescues of persons who had fallen in the river below the falls. There were twenty-seven reports for rescues on Difficult Run of people who had been swept away in the stream and no reports of suspicious accidents. Since all of the incidents on Difficult Run had occurred during daytime hours, M.J. disregarded them entirely.

She thanked Becky again, picked up the copies of the reports from the Fairfax County Police files and drove back to the park. It was late in the afternoon when she arrived and Dodd was paging through one of the logs.

"Ten left to go," he said. "How'd you make out?"

She told him about the three suspicious missing person reports she had found. "They fit the pattern," she said. "Did you find anything?"

"Well, no suspicious accidents or missing people, but I did find something that's interesting," he said. "In early April 1970 a call came into the office from a man. He and his wife had been out walking on Difficult Run the night before. They heard something moving through the woods north of the trail and when they looked they saw what they thought was a bear. Couldn't shine their flashlight to get a better look because the batteries had gone dead, but there was a pretty bright moon shining through the trees." Dodd paused. "Now here's what got my attention: The man said that whatever it was turned and looked at them and when it did the face didn't look like a bear at all, more like a gorilla. That's when they decided to head back to their car."

"Could it have been a bear?" M.J. asked.

"Well, we do get bears in the park sometimes, but not usually until later in the year," Dodd replied. "I think what they saw was an ape."

"That incident just made me realize something," M.J. said. "I've been trying to figure out what causes the attacks. I thought it might just be inherent aggressive behavior, but I think there's another explanation. All of the victims had some sort of light with them—a flashlight, a lantern or, in the case of the boys, helmet lights. That makes sense because it was dark, but I think that's what causes the ape to attack. I just remembered that Ollie Coppin talked about boys shining lights in the ape's eyes and how it became enraged, bared its teeth and shook the cage. I'd be willing to bet that if that couple's flashlight had worked, they'd have been attacked too."

"That makes sense," Dodd said. "But I've been wondering about something else too. All of the victims except the boys and Doc wound up in the stream. Do you think this thing throws them in after it kills them?"

"I've given that a lot of thought," M.J. said. "I don't think it throws them in. I think they're trying to get away from it and their body falls in after they're killed, just like what probably happened to Kevin Murphy in 1942. The reason we found the boys on the trail was because they were on bikes and the best route of escape seemed to be to ride away. In Doc's case, I think Lola may have attacked first and Doc was trying to help her instead of running away himself."

She continued, "Put yourself in the position of the victims: You are walking or standing on Difficult Run at night. You hear something nearby and instinctively shine whatever kind of light you're carrying in that direction. Then two things happen at the same time: The ape becomes enraged and you see what it is. You become frightened and look for a way to escape. The stream seems like the best way to go under the circumstances because staying on the trail guarantees that it will come after you, but maybe if you can get into the water, or, even better, to the far bank, it may not follow you. The problem is that when you turn to flee you expose your back to the ape and it pounces on you and breaks your neck."

"God," Dodd said, "what a horrible way to die."

"It certainly is," M.J. responded. "That's why we've got to find these things and either capture or kill them. As I see it, there are only two more questions we need to answer: Why do these attacks all seem to have occurred at the same time of year and where do the apes live?"

It was getting late in the day and M.J. offered to stay and help Dodd go through the remaining log books. "Thanks for offering," Dodd said, "but it would probably take you longer to decipher all the entries. I can finish these off in about an hour because I know what I'm looking for."

"In that case," she said, "I'm going to stop by my office and then head to my apartment. I'll see you in the morning."

As M.J. was driving down the GW, her cell phone rang. It was Jake.

"So, what's going on with the murder cases?" he asked.

"If you buy me some pizza and beer, I'll fill you in," M.J. replied.

"Sure. Anything else?" he asked.

"Anything else on the case or anything besides pizza and beer?" she asked with a laugh.

"Well, I was hoping for something else after we eat." he said.

"We'll see, but I'm really tired. I'll meet you at the pizza place about seven thirty," M.J. said.

When she arrived, Jake had already secured a table and ordered two beers. M.J. gave him a kiss on the cheek, sat down and took a long drink of beer.

"So what's going on with the cases?" he asked.

"I'm going to tell you, but I want you to promise you'll keep it to yourself for now," M.J. said. "I haven't filed any more reports and I don't plan to until I tie up some more loose ends."

"I promise," he said. "Sounds pretty mysterious."

She began telling him about everything that had happened since the murders of Doc and Lola. Jake sat quietly, taking it all in. He ordered another round of beers after about thirty minutes.

When M.J. had finished, Jake said, "Wow! If that's who—or should I say *what*—committed these murders then it's the longest running serial killing case in history."

"I hadn't thought about it that way, but I guess it would be," she replied, smiling.

"What can I do to help?" he asked.

"Nothing right now," she replied, "but when I pull the rest of the pieces together, I may need to get you involved.

Mostly, I'm going to need you to back me up on this when I have to take it to Swain."

"Not a problem," he said. "Let's order some pizza."

After they ate and were walking back to their cars, Jake asked, "So, can I come over tonight?"

M.J. thought for a moment, then said, "Sure. That would be nice. But don't expect me to be great company. It's been a long couple of days. I'll also warn you that I'll be getting up really early."

"I think I can handle all of that," Jake replied. "I'll see you at your place."

CHAPTER TWENTY-SIX

M.J. left quietly the next morning to keep from waking Jake, who was sleeping soundly. As she drove to Great Falls Park, she thought about the night before and was glad that she had spent it with him. They had made love and then cuddled while they slept, which had given her a sense of refuge from the events of the last few days. She realized that the idea of moving in with him no longer seemed so foreign.

On her morning run she once again found herself scanning the forest, but this time the landscape seemed decidedly more foreboding. She imagined the figure of an ape, crouched and moving slowly and cautiously through the underbrush, stopping occasionally to listen for sounds of the humans that it sought to avoid. It occurred to her that even such a large animal could move through the forest unnoticed in broad daylight, although she remained convinced that the apes had long ago become night creatures to eliminate human contact altogether. She wondered how it would be possible to track such an animal, much less capture it. After all, Dr. Peterson had made three trips to the Congo without ever even seeing one. Would it be any easier for him or anyone else to find one now in the dense forest of Great Falls Park?

She recalled Peterson saying that during his trips he had been shown droppings that supposedly came from the Bili Ape. Even assuming these traces could be found in the expanse of Great Falls Park, she knew they would not provide the type of proof she needed. First and foremost, there would be no way to prove that the droppings were actually those of an ape. She could just see herself marching into Swain's office and tossing an evidence bag filled with excrement on his desk. *Lieutenant, I've solved the case! This is a bag of ape shit!* Just visualizing the scene made her start laughing. No, she would have to find a way to prove the existence of the apes that could not be questioned and right now she was not sure what that would be.

She showered, changed and went to Dodd's office. He was sitting at the conference room table with a chart spread out in front of him. He glanced up with an excited look on his face.

"M.J., I think I may have figured something out," he said. "The fact that all of the murders occurred in the spring was really bugging me, so I stayed late last night to research what else might have been going on when they occurred. I started with the date of the earliest incident that you found that would still be covered by our records—that would be April 16, 1972. When I looked at the entries around that date it showed that for that entire week the river was at flood stage, so high that it came all the way into the park. So I checked the entries around all of the other incidents and, sure enough, each time the river was at flood stage. Not always enough to flood the main park, but enough to fill up Mather Gorge to its rim.   Then it dawned on me that Kevin Murphy was murdered in the spring of 1942, right after a huge flood here. We don't have records going back that far, but 1942 is one of the marks on the post out by the overlook that I showed you—just below the one for the Great Flood of 1936.

"Here, take a look at this," he said, pointing to the chart on the table. "This is a graph of the daily river depth going back to 1966. The horizontal red line shows the depth that would be flood stage. I put a notation by the dates for each incident, including the couple that probably saw an ape in the forest. You can see that they all occurred when the river was way up."

M.J. bent over the chart and ran her finger down the red horizontal line. "What do you think it means?" she asked.

"I think it means the apes live somewhere in the cliffs along Mather Gorge," Dodd said. "When the river gets high enough, they have to leave their nest and move to some place that's not flooded. I believe that place is Difficult Run. If you think about it, Difficult Run is a miniature version of the gorge—a stream, plenty of rocks and not a lot of human activity, especially at night."

"But where in Mather Gorge?" M.J. asked.

"That I don't know, but let's take a little trip and see if we can figure it out," he said, handing M.J. a pair of binoculars from a shelf and taking a pair for himself.

They took Dodd's SUV and drove to the C&O Canal National Historic Park located in Maryland, across the Potomac from Great Falls Park. They walked from the parking lot over the bridge to Bear Island, which formed the northeast boundary of Mather Gorge, then followed a rugged path called, appropriately, the Billy Goat Trail to about the midway point in the gorge. There was a ledge above the trail that was a good place to sit and view the rock walls on the other side of the river.

M.J. looked through her binoculars and slowly surveyed the cliff on the Virginia side of the gorge. This section of the gorge was easily a mile long and contained hundreds of crevices and cave-like openings.

"They could be living in any one of those openings," she said.

"Well, I think most likely they're using one toward the southern end of the gorge to stay away from people. The rock climbers are mostly confined to that area," he said, pointing upstream toward a higher section of the cliff.

"Even so," M.J. replied, "they could be anywhere over there."

"I'm afraid you're right, but at least we can concentrate on just one area of the park," Dodd said.

Suddenly, M.J. blurted out, "We need a trail camera! Like the one that was used to take the picture of the ape I showed you."

"That just might work," Dodd replied enthusiastically, "but I don't think these things probably stick to a trail. Besides, we can't put it anywhere that a hiker might see it and take it home as a souvenir." He thought for a moment. "They probably forage back in the forest along the rim of the gorge. There's a little meadow right over there," he said, pointing at a spot downriver about a hundred yards. "It would be a good place for the camera. Nice open field of view and back far enough from the trail that hikers wouldn't see it."

They went back to Dodd's SUV and, instead of returning directly to the park, drove to a shopping mall just off the Capital Beltway that had a large sporting goods store. In the section devoted to hunting gear they found an area with an array of trail cameras.

Dodd examined the specifications on several of the packages, then picked one up and said, "This is what we need. Motion activated, infrared flash, programmable. We'd better get some extra batteries and another memory card too."

They drove back to Great Falls Park and took the camera into Dodd's office, being careful to close the door. Dodd took the camera out of its box, inserted the batteries, briefly looked at the instructions and began adjusting the settings. "There, that should do it," he said after a few minutes. "It's programmed to only take pictures between dusk and dawn. The range is only about forty feet, but anything that moves in that area will have its picture taken. Let's take it out to the site."

He placed the camera in a small backpack and they walked down to the section of the River Trail that ran along Mather Gorge. At the southern end of the trail, they looked around to make sure there were no hikers, then left the trail and walked into the forest. As Dodd had said, there was a small meadow, perhaps one hundred feet wide and about fifty feet deep. The ground cover was wild grass about a foot high and a rock outcropping ran along the entire back of the open area.

They strapped the camera around a tree on the side of the meadow closest to the gorge and aimed it toward the open area. Dodd pressed a small switch on its side and said, "It's ready to go. We can come and get the memory card in the morning, replace it with the spare and see what we got."

The next morning, M.J. went to the park and, instead of running, hiked to the meadow and removed the memory card from the camera, replacing it with the spare. She went back to Dodd's office and he loaded the card into the reader on his computer. There were six images, all of deer grazing in the meadow.

The infrared flash gave the scenes an eerie quality. Although the foreground was fairly vivid, animals beyond the forty-foot range of the flash appeared as shadowy images, except for the eyes of those looking in the direction of the camera, which appeared as bright dots.

They repeated this routine on the following days. There were more images of deer, an occasional fox, and a mother raccoon being followed by her three babies. On the third day, there was an image of a pack of coyotes, causing Dodd to remark, "Well, I guess that confirms the sightings that have been reported."

That afternoon, M.J. stopped by the National Zoo on her way back to Anacostia Station. She parked, walked to the Great Ape House and entered the area that housed the gorillas. She had come, she decided, because she wanted a better sense of just what she was dealing with. After all, this was not a case where you could do a background check on the suspect, perhaps ponder a mug shot or interview some acquaintances.

She went to the glassed-in area that housed the Western Lowland Gorillas. One was sitting on an artificial tree in the back of the enclosure, pondering the visitors lined up along the glass barrier. People were taking pictures with cameras and cell phones and M.J. wondered why the flashes didn't produce the same angry reaction in the gorilla that she believed had caused the attacks on Difficult Run. Then she realized that the gorillas in the zoo had never lived in the

wild and were, for all intents and purposes, domesticated—
they had grown up having lights flashed in their faces.

The gorilla left its perch and ambled down to the glass
barrier. It stopped right in front of M.J. and looked directly
into her eyes. She returned the gaze and in that moment
realized that this was a thinking creature, perhaps closer to
human than animal. *This*, she thought, *is what the killer is
like*, and it caused her to feel a small shiver.

By the fourth day, M.J. was beginning to lose hope that
the trail camera would produce a picture of an ape. She
removed the memory card and took it to Dodd's office.
There were more pictures of deer grazing in the meadow and
they scrolled through the familiar scenes.

Suddenly, Dodd said, "Wait a minute, what's that?"

Behind the grazing deer was a dark shape atop the rock
outcropping, just beyond the range of the full flash. Its eyes
appeared as two bright spots. Dodd enlarged that portion of
the image.

The grainy outline of a figure was clearly visible and it
looked like an ape walking on all fours across the rocks—
what M.J. recalled from her visit to the zoo was known as
"knuckle walking."

"That's what I've been waiting for," she said.

CHAPTER TWENTY-SEVEN

M.J. continued going to the park every morning, retrieving the memory card from the trail camera and, together with Dodd, looking at the images from the night before in the hope that there would be a better picture of an ape. After that, she would usually go for a run, shower and change, and drive to Anacostia Station to work on what she hoped would be her final report on the murder cases.

One afternoon, she received a call from Dodd. "Doc's funeral is going to be the day after tomorrow at 10:00 a.m.," he said. "Sorry for such short notice, but another funeral got postponed and my friend at Arlington National Cemetery got Doc's put on the schedule in its place. I'm going to keep just a couple of rangers here at the park and everybody else plans on attending."

"You know I'll be there; my partner Jake, too," she replied.

On the day of the funeral, she and Jake put on their dress blue uniforms and drove together to Arlington. Six sailors in dress whites lined up as pallbearers and carried the flag-draped casket to the gravesite. A Navy chaplain said a few words about Doc's service to his country and how he had been taken from this life by a senseless act. He exhorted everyone to remember his life as one of sacrifice for his fellow man.

M.J. stood by the grave listening to the chaplain, but thinking about Doc and Lola. When taps was played by a lone bugler, M.J. saluted along with everyone else, but found herself crying quietly. Dodd, who stood next to her, also had tears rolling down his face, as did several of the rangers.

At the conclusion of the service, the flag was folded by the sailors and the chaplain brought it to M.J. and Dodd. They received it together, but Dodd turned to M.J. and said, "You take this . . . Doc and Lola would want you to have it." She hugged Dodd and put the flag firmly under her arm. "Thank you," she said.

Jake drove M.J. back to her apartment. She carefully placed the folded flag in a dresser drawer, changed out of her dress uniform and into her work clothes, and left for Anacostia Station.

She was on her third draft of the report, which was close to forty pages long, not including attached copies of Fairfax County Police reports, Fire and Rescue reports, autopsy reports, crime scene pictures, Zerk's forensic reports, the picture provided by Dr. Peterson, and the trail camera picture.   She had decided that unless the trail camera produced a better picture of an ape in the next few days, she was going to file the report and ask for a meeting with Swain.

By the end of the week, the trail camera had taken close to fifty more pictures, none of which included an ape.   M.J. worked late Friday and into the night on Saturday.   She finished the report early Sunday morning and called Jake around 6:00 a.m.

"I'll buy you breakfast.   Pick you up in fifteen minutes," she said.

She brought a copy of the report with her and handed it to Jake.   "Here's some homework for you," she said.   "When we're finished eating, I'd like for you to take it to your apartment and read it.   I'll check in later and you can tell me what you think."

She dropped Jake off at his apartment and went to hers to take a much-needed nap.   She woke up around 4:00 p.m. and called Jake.   He had finished reading the report and she went over to his apartment.

"Well, what do you think?" she asked.

"You did a great job, M.J.," he said. "I don't know what else you could have put in the report. It's still going to be a tough sell with Swain, but you have to try anyway."

"I know that," she replied. "I plan to turn it in tomorrow morning and ask for a meeting after he's read it. I want you to come to the meeting, too, and back me up."

"You know I will," he said, looking at his watch. "How about an early dinner—on me?"

"It's a deal," she said.

By unspoken agreement, they did not discuss the cases or the report during dinner.   Instead, they concentrated on enjoying each other's company, which included small talk about their families and friends. After dinner, they returned to Jake's apartment where they spent the night together.

M.J. arose before dawn the next morning, returned to her apartment, showered and changed into her work clothes. She arrived at Anacostia Station before roll call and handed a copy of the report to Tony Lauretta.

"This is for the Lieutenant," she said. "Jake and I would like to meet with him after he's read it."

"Well, if investigations were measured by the pound," he said, hefting the report, "this has to be one of the most thorough I've ever been handed. I'll let you guys know about the meeting."

After roll call, M.J. drove to the park, went running and retrieved the memory card from the trail camera on her way back to the Visitor Center. After showering and changing clothes, she stopped by Dodd's office and they looked at the pictures from the night before. There were only pictures of more deer, two foxes, and a large owl that had flown by the camera.

"I turned in my report this morning," she told Dodd. "Probably meet with the Lieutenant tomorrow."

"I hope that goes well," Dodd said. "We need to do something before there's another murder. I even thought about taking this up through Park Service channels myself, but they would just say it's a police matter. Might even call your Lieutenant and piss him off."

"I think you're right about that. He's not the kind that would appreciate having somebody try to cut around him," she replied. "Besides, it's my case and my problem for now. No reason to hang your ass out yet. I'll let you know how it goes tomorrow."

The next morning, Tony Lauretta came up to M.J. and Jake before roll call. "Lieutenant wants to meet with you guys at ten," he said.

"Did you read the report, Tony?" M.J. asked.

"I did," he responded.

"What did you think of it?" M.J. asked.

"Well, M.J., it's really something and a fine piece of detective work," he said, "but that's just my opinion and the Lieutenant has the final say."

"I know that, Tony, but I appreciate your opinion," M.J. replied.

At ten o'clock she and Jake went into Swain's office. He was sitting behind his desk and motioned them to the two chairs in front of it. The report was lying on the desk in front of him.

"I read your report very carefully. It's a hell of a story," he said. "Let me ask you this, though: Even if everything in it is true, isn't this a job for Fairfax County Animal Control?" He wasn't smiling.

M.J. was incredulous.

"Animal Control! Animal Control!" she exclaimed. "This isn't a raccoon caught in a chimney or the neighbor's dog shitting on someone's lawn. This is a creature that's killed three people on our watch and God knows how many before that!"

"Now calm down, Detective," Swain said. "Let's take a look at the evidence you've got—and I think you'll agree it's all pretty circumstantial. This whole theory of yours started with a story about two apes released into the forest in Great Falls Park in what"—he paged through the report—"1936. Then you've got a suspicious death in 1942 where the M.E. is second-guessing the county coroner and says it's the same cause of death we've been dealing with in the last year."

"It's also consistent with the way these apes kill their enemies," M.J. interjected.

"That may be true," Swain continued, "but it still assumes the 1942 death was from the same cause as the recent ones. It also assumes that this ape—or its ancestor—was the killer in both cases. That's a lot of assumptions."

"But what about all of the unexplained deaths in between?" M.J. asked.

"Well, I don't agree that all of those deaths are unexplained or at least unexplainable," Swain replied. "Working backwards, you've got an amateur ornithologist that the EMS guys said broke his neck when he fell into some rocks—and, of course, he was cremated, so we can't confirm your theory with an autopsy. Then you've got some drunks who were probably so tanked that they fell in the water and drowned, a photographer from the city who didn't know his way around in the woods, and a couple of fishermen who probably got their lures caught on something, went in to retrieve them and got swept away in the current—hell, I'm always having to go after lures when I fish."

"But what about the sightings and the picture?" M.J. asked impatiently.

"Let's see," Swain said. "You've got a sighting of some dark figure in the woods by a homeless Vietnam vet, who was probably drunk at the time . . ."

"Doc didn't drink," M.J. interrupted.

"Be that as it may," Swain continued, "he could have just seen some guy wearing a hooded sweatshirt out in the rain. And by the way, Detective, you were allowing that guy to camp illegally on federal park land—we'll be talking about that later."

"And what about the couple that saw an ape-like creature on Difficult Run?" M.J. asked.

"They reported that they saw a bear and it probably was a bear," Swain said. "I think they just imagined the gorilla face."

"But there's a trail camera picture!" M.J. exclaimed.

"There's a trail camera picture of *something*, I'll grant you that, but it's hard to say what it is. It could be a bear," Swain replied.

"It's too early in the year for bears to be in the park and bears don't walk that way," M.J. said.

"Look, Detective, the picture is just of the outline of something on a rock. I don't think you or anybody else can say for sure what it is," Swain said. "Now, what are you recommending that we do?"

"Close the park and get some people in there who know how to track these things and either capture or kill them," M.J. replied.

"That, Detective, would require that I go up through our chain of command to the Chief, who would then have to go to the Director of the Park Service and tell him that we think Bigfoot is loose in Great Falls Park . . . and that's not going to happen," Swain said. He paused. "Jake, I haven't heard anything from you. What do you think about all of this?"

Jake cleared his throat and said, "Well, I think you've got some good points there, Lieutenant."

M.J. turned and scowled at Jake.

Swain nodded and continued, "Here's the bottom line: You've got thirty days to either come up with some better proof of your theory or find another solution. After that, I'm going to try and palm this off on the FBI and get it off my desk. That's it for now." He stood to signal the end of the meeting.

M.J. and Jake stood, but before leaving M.J. said, "If we don't do something now, Lieutenant, more people are going to be murdered and we'll be responsible for it."

Swain didn't reply and M.J. and Jake left his office, closing the door behind them.

Outside, M.J. turned to Jake and said "Thanks for backing me up, you prick!"

She turned to walk away and Jake said, "But M.J., I . . . "

She didn't wait for him to finish.

CHAPTER TWENTY-EIGHT

M.J. drove to Great Falls Park and went running. She pushed herself for a full six miles, a lot of it uphill. By the time she returned to the locker room, she had calmed, but hadn't eliminated, the anger she felt toward Swain and Jake. In the case of Jake, she thought, there was also an equal measure of hurt feelings and disappointment. He had completely let her down and she didn't think she could ever forgive him for that.

As soon as she entered Dodd's office, she remembered that she had forgotten to get the memory card from the camera.

"I forgot to check the camera," she said. "I'll go back and get the memory card."

Dodd noticed that she seemed upset and said, "I'll walk with you and you can tell me what happened this morning."

As they walked toward Mather Gorge, she told him about the meeting with Swain and the thirty-day ultimatum.

"Damn!" he said. "Well, all we can do is keep checking the camera and hope for a break."

They swapped memory cards and went back to Dodd's office. The pictures from the night before were of the usual collection of park animals, but no ape.

When M.J. arrived for roll call the next morning, someone had placed a toy gorilla on her desk and when she sat down its eyes started flashing and its arms started beating its chest. She could hear muffled laughter from the other cubicles—all male. She wanted to stand up and start yelling obscenities, but decided against it. Instead, she turned off the toy and unceremoniously dropped it in her wastebasket.

Tony Lauretta appeared at the entrance to her cubicle. "What the hell's going on M.J.?" he asked.

She pointed to her wastebasket and said, "Some of the guys thought that would be cute."

Lauretta leaned down and picked up the toy gorilla. At roll call, he held it up and said, "One of you kids seems to have lost a toy. Now I'm going to keep it for you so you don't hurt yourself on any of the moving parts." He paused and said, "If any of you think this was funny, I'm here to tell you that this was one of the most unprofessional things I've ever seen and totally disrespectful of a fellow officer. If anything like this happens again, you'll be dealing with me. Is that understood?"

They all nodded their heads and none of the male officers, except Jake, would even look at M.J. All of the women officers looked her way and smiled.

After roll call, Jake came up and tried to talk to M.J. She turned and walked away.

M.J. went to Tony Lauretta's desk and thanked him. "Don't mention it," he said, "just doing my job." As she turned to leave, he added, "You're a good detective, M.J. You keep on this."

The trail camera produced nothing of use for the next week and M.J. and Dodd were becoming more discouraged with each passing day. When M.J. went to the park the following morning, the sky was becoming overcast and as she entered Dodd's office he said, "We may have a problem developing. I just checked the weather reports and there's a large storm that's been stalled for almost two days over what they call the Potomac Highlands—that's a large area in Virginia, West Virginia and Western Maryland that feeds the river. It's dropping one to two inches of rain an hour and if that keeps up we'll have flooding down here for sure."

"How long before that happens?" she asked.

"The River Desk at the National Weather Service says we should start to see the river rising late this afternoon and that it will probably reach flood stage late tonight or early tomorrow morning," he replied.

"Can I check back with you later today?" she asked.

"Sure," he replied.

M.J. drove to Anacostia Station and shuffled through some papers on her desk, not really reading any of them. Just after four in the afternoon, she called Dodd.

"What's the latest on the river?" she asked.

"Well, it's come up quite a bit already," he replied. "The River Desk says flood stage will start about 2 a.m."

"How about Mather Gorge?" she asked.

"Oh, it'll be to the top a lot earlier, midnight at the latest," he said.

She thanked him for the information.

"M.J.," he said, "don't do anything stupid."

"Don't worry, I won't," she replied. "See you tomorrow."

She sat at her desk thinking for a while, then walked to Jake's desk and found the Nikon camera he kept in one of its drawers. He had already gone for the day, so she left a note on his desktop that said "Borrowed your camera – M.J."

She went to her apartment and microwaved a frozen dinner. When she had finished eating about half of it, she lay down on her bed and set the alarm.

The alarm went off at 1:00 a.m. and she went into her bathroom and splashed some cold water on her face, put on her hiking shoes and looked outside. It was drizzling, so she found her black rain slicker. Before she put it on, she checked the ammo magazine in her gun and the two spares she carried on her belt.

There was almost no traffic on the drive to the Difficult Run parking lot, which was empty. She put the camera strap around her neck and zipped up the rain slicker, then opened the trunk of her car and removed a heavy flashlight from its bracket. It was still drizzling and the cloud cover was thick enough to obscure all but occasional glints of moonlight. She switched on the flashlight and started toward Difficult Run.

She alternated between illuminating the trail and the wooded hillside to her left with the flashlight, walking slowly enough to sweep the beam back and forth several times every few feet. It took her close to an hour to reach the end of the trail where the stream emptied into the Potomac. She could hear the water crashing against the rock walls that lined the right-angle turn at the bottom of Mather Gorge.

She had not seen or heard anything on her walk down the trail. *This may be the stupidest thing I've ever done*, she thought. *Maybe Swain was right and there isn't any ape. Maybe I just started looking at everything through one filter and made it come out the way I wanted.*

She sighed, turned and started back up the trail, shining the light to the right as she went. She had gone about a hundred feet when she thought she heard something ahead of her on the trail. She raised the flashlight and could see a dark figure in the mist coming down the trail toward her. When it came fully into the beam of the flashlight, she could see an ape, knuckle-walking slowly with its head raised and its eyes looking directly at her. These were not the soft, human eyes of the zoo gorilla. These eyes were filled with rage.

When the ape was about thirty feet away from her, it stopped walking and stood upright, baring its teeth. It was huge, easily as tall as she was, and showed no sign of stopping its advance. The flashlight shining in its eyes obviously enraged it, but M.J. was not about to shine the beam elsewhere.

M.J. kept the flashlight in her left hand with her left arm extended laterally. She drew her gun with her right hand and thought to herself, *Now what, stupid? Stop while I take your picture! Put your hands up! Stop or I'll shoot!* She aimed the gun, took the safety off and put her finger on the trigger.

The ape had dropped back down to its knuckle-walking position, but when it got about ten feet away from M.J. it rose back up, extended its arms and looked ready to leap.

M.J. fired once and hit the ape mid-chest. It looked down in amazement and placed one of its fingers against the entrance wound, then examined its blood-smeared finger. It let out a high-pitched scream and then started to run toward M.J.

M.J. fired a second time and the ape fell backwards onto the trail. It seemed to take a few labored breaths and then stopped moving altogether.

M.J. moved closer, keeping both the flashlight and the gun aimed at the ape. When she felt confident that the ape was dead, she holstered her gun and reached inside her rain slicker for the camera. She raised it and pushed the shutter button. Nothing happened. She tried again. Nothing. "Shit!" she said aloud and put the camera back inside the slicker.

She was still standing with the flashlight examining the ape's body, when she heard something drop heavily onto the trail behind her. She drew her gun and spun around, still holding the flashlight in her extended left hand.

It was another ape. It had apparently jumped down from the rock outcropping next to the trail and was standing fully upright just a few feet from M.J., its teeth bared and a look of pure hatred on its face. It was much taller than the one M.J. had just killed, easily six feet, maybe more.

Before M.J. could fire, the ape extended its left arm and swung with such force that it knocked the gun out of her hand. It followed with its right hand and the flashlight went flying into the rock wall.

The flashlight had stayed on and there was enough reflected light for M.J. to see that the ape was advancing slowly. She backed away, knowing that to turn around would cause the ape to leap onto her back and kill her. Her right heel touched the body of the dead ape and she cautiously stepped around it. When the advancing ape reached the body, it stopped for a moment and looked down. That was all that M.J. needed. She spun around and started running up the trail.

She was certain that her right wrist was broken and it dangled uselessly by her side. She put the pain out of her mind and concentrated on distancing herself from the ape, which she could hear running on all fours on the hard-packed trail behind her. Then she didn't hear the sound of the ape's running for a few seconds and suddenly it could be heard again, only this time closer. *It's going over the rock outcroppings to shorten the distance between us*, she thought.

She knew she dare not look around to see just how closely she was being pursued. The trail was almost completely dark except for the moonlight that occasionally shone through the rain clouds. She knew she had to remain completely focused and try to stay as near the center of the trail as possible.

She was running as fast as she could manage with her crippled wrist. She figured her pace was probably slightly better than the ape's, but she could not let up for an instant. Somewhere in the back of her mind, she recalled seeing a gaping wound on the ape's right arm just before it knocked the flashlight out of her hand. *Lola!*, she thought, and that thought gave her the energy to increase her pace.

She guessed that she was perhaps a hundred yards from the end of the trail, maybe less. What would she do next? There was a shotgun in the trunk of her car, but she had no hope of getting to it. The car keys were in her pocket, but, even if she could get to them, the odds of opening the trunk fast enough to grab the shotgun were slim. Besides, even if she got the gun, how could she use it with just one arm? If she continued straight on the trail, it would take her onto Georgetown Pike. Maybe a passing motorist would see her and stop to help. *Passing cars at almost three in the morning? Probably no cars at all*, she thought.

A tree limb had fallen across the trail and she reached it just as the moon completely disappeared behind the clouds. She didn't see it and her right foot struck it, causing her to tumble forward and land on her injured wrist. She let out a sharp cry of pain and tried to lift herself up using her left arm.

It was too late. The beast landed on her back, causing her to crash to the ground. Its hands immediately clamped onto the sides of her head. She stiffened her neck and shoulder muscles to counter the ape's effort to pull her head back and twist it, but the force was so great that she was losing the battle and she felt her head come back and start to turn.

Suddenly, she saw a bright flash of light and heard a loud pop! *So this is what it's like to have your neck broken*, she thought. *Next, I guess I'll get to see my grandma.*

Instead, she felt the pressure release on her head and the full weight of the ape's limp body fall onto her back. She stayed motionless for a moment and then the ape rolled off to her left side.

She raised herself up on her right side. It took a few seconds for her eyes to adjust, but when they did she saw Jake standing next to the ape holding a flashlight and a gun.

He prodded the ape's body with his foot and, when there was no response, holstered the gun and reached into his pocket. He pulled out four AA batteries which he held up and said, "You forgot the batteries for the camera."

CHAPTER TWENTY-NINE

Jake helped M.J. to his car and took her to the hospital. On the way, he called the GW Station and asked them to send some uniformed officers to secure Difficult Run.

"Have them get in touch with Dr. Julia Matheson at the National Zoo," M.J. said. "They need to tell her there are two large, dead apes that need to be picked up. I think she'll understand. Oh, and have them retrieve my gun and flashlight, please."

It turned out that Dodd had tried to reach M.J. on her cell phone around midnight to give her an update on the flooding. When he couldn't reach her—she later discovered her cell phone batteries were dead—he had become worried and had reached Jake through Dispatch a little after 1:00 a.m. to share his concerns. Jake had tried M.J.'s apartment phone and, when she didn't answer, had gone to Anacostia to look for her. He had seen the note on his desk, immediately figured out what was going on and driven to Difficult Run, arriving there just before 3:00 a.m. He had seen M.J.'s car in the parking lot, gotten out of his car and, just as he was starting down the trail, heard two shots echoing off the rock walls along the valley. As he had begun running down the trail, he had heard M.J. cry out—not too far ahead of where he was—and had drawn his gun, arriving just in time to kill the ape.

At the hospital, the doctors determined that M.J.'s wrist wasn't broken, just badly sprained. It was put in a rigid wrap and she was given some pain medication. Jake took her to her apartment and put her to bed. He gave her some of the pain medication and kissed her on the forehead.

Just before M.J. closed her eyes, she said, "You're still a prick, you know."

"I know, but a lovable prick nonetheless," he replied and quietly closed her bedroom door. He spent the night on her couch. When she awoke in the morning he served her breakfast in bed.

"You stay here today. I'll fill them in at the office about what happened," he said.

"No argument from me," she said and went back to sleep.

The next morning, Jake drove her to Anacostia Station for roll call. When they entered, everyone stood and began clapping. Even Swain appeared with a sheepish grin on his face and joined in the applause. Tony Lauretta came over and put his arm around her shoulders. "Good work, M.J.," he said.

They had ordered a fancy pastry and had it decorated with "M.J. Powers—Super Detective." Someone brought her a cup of coffee and the first slice of pastry. As she was eating it, the phone rang. Someone picked it up and said, "M.J., it's for you."

"I'll just take it back here," she said, walking into her cubicle. "Hello, this is Detective Powers."

"Detective, this is Dr. Matheson at the National Zoo," the voice said. "Steve Peterson from National Geographic is here with me. We just finished the autopsies on the apes. They are definitely Bilis. The bigger one is a male and the smaller one is a female. There's something else you should know, Detective . . . the female has given birth twice."

M.J. was quiet for a few seconds and then said, "I see, Doctor.   Thank   you,"   and   hung   up   the   phone.

EPILOGUE

Based on M.J.'s encounters with the apes on Difficult Run and Dr. Matheson's autopsy findings, the Park Police recommended to the Director of the National Park Service that Great Falls Park be closed until the remaining animals could be found and either captured or killed.

The official reason for the closure of the park was given as "major trail and facility renovations." The main entrance gate was kept locked and a uniformed Park Police officer was stationed at the entrance to Difficult Run to prevent access to the park from that direction.

A Park Police SWAT team was assigned to positions in the forest along Mather Gorge from sundown until sunrise. They were equipped with night vision goggles and tranquilizer rifles provided by the National Zoo.

After a week, the SWAT team members spotted the two apes in the forest—not far from the meadow where M.J. and Dodd had placed the trail camera. They were able to fire tranquilizer darts into both animals, which were then taken to a temporary enclosure at the National Zoo's Conservation and Research Center in Front Royal, Virginia. Dr. Matheson determined that the male was about ten years old and the female about six years old, and that the female was too immature to have produced any offspring.

M.J. and Jake met with the parents of the two murdered boys to explain the circumstances surrounding their deaths. After the initial shock of learning that their sons had been killed by an animal, they expressed a sense of relief in knowing that the murders were not the act of a deranged human. They thanked M.J. and Jake for bringing some degree of closure to this tragedy in their lives.

In late 2006, the Bili apes were moved to a permanent facility at the National Zoo adjacent to the Great Ape House. Once the facility was opened to the public, signs were placed all along the viewing area that said FLASH PHOTOGRAPHY STRICTLY PROHIBITED.

M.J. was presented with a commendation medal. She never visited the National Zoo to see the captive apes.

Acknowledgements

By its very nature, writing is a solitary endeavor. But along the way, and after a book is finished, writers rely on information, advice, criticism and support that can only come from others. With that in mind, I would like to thank the following:

My wonderful wife, Nikki, who has been my advisor and loving critic throughout; Karen Washburn, resident historian of Great Falls for her advice, historical and otherwise; Lieutenant Commander John Childs, Medical Corps, USN for his invaluable advice on medical details; John Weldin for his tutoring on the finer points of distance running; Captain Thomas Neider for providing technical advice as well as insights into the day-to-day activities and culture of the U.S. Park Police; and all of the instructors at the U.S. Park Police Citizens' Academy for reminding me what it means to be a law enforcement officer.

Dee Jessee and Julia Matheson who read multiple copies of the manuscript and gave thoughtful suggestions and encouragement with each reading; Steve Peterson, Viddy Comsa, Rosalie Peterson and Lawrence Martinelli who were kind enough to read the manuscript and give me their honest appraisal; and my dog, Noochie, who hiked hundreds of miles with me through Great Falls Park while I was writing the book in my head.

A very special thanks to Sarah Mishler, editor extraordinaire.

Lastly, I owe a debt of gratitude to the late Marian Reed and Milburn Sanders for their recollections of growing up in Great Falls.

Catherine Tyler

About the Author

John Dibble is an attorney in Washington, D.C. He has served as a special assistant to a U.S. senator, a commanding officer in the U.S. Navy, and a prosecuting attorney. He currently serves as Chairman of the Vietnam Veterans Memorial Fund, which built and maintains the Wall on the National Mall.

He lives in Great Falls, Virginia with his wife and daughter.